D1051371

"Stephen Turner is dead," I said. "Look at it this way. Somebody went to a lot of effort and expense to kill him. Why? All I'm asking is for you to tell me if there's anything at all that you know or have heard that might give me a reason." I reached across the table and took her hand. "You said you loved him, once. You owe him something."

Deborah finished her drink and stood up. "I'm going home. Stay here. I'll call you in the morning."

I slept badly. At four in the morning the phone rang twice, stopped, then rang again.

"Riordan?" It was Deborah Greene. "Oh my God, I'm sorry, we've got to talk. It's about Joshua. It was so long ago, but it could be connected with Steve's death. . . ."

THE JOSHUA SEQUENCE

Fredrick D. Huebner

FAWCETT GOLD MEDAL • NEW YORK

A Fawcett Gold Medal Book
Published by Ballantine Books
Copyright © 1986 by Fredrick D. Huebner

All rights reserved under International and Pan-American Copyright
Conventions. Published in the United States by Ballantine Books, a division
of Random House, Inc., New York, and simultaneously in Canada by
Random House of Canada Limited, Toronto.

Library of Congress Catalog Card Number: 86-91185

ISBN 0-449-13128-9

All the characters in this book are fictitious, and any resemblance to
persons living or dead is purely coincidental.

Manufactured in the United States of America

First Edition: November 1986

CHAPTER 1

The day they shot down Stephen Turner was the last good day of Indian summer. The afternoon that day was full of warm, hazy sunlight, the color of old yellowed satin, and the cafés that lined the brick streets of the Pioneer Square district were still full at three o'clock. Now and then a wind with the cold stone heart of November in it drifted up from the waterfront. The drinkers in the cafés shivered and reached for their glasses, then pulled up their collars and tugged down their sleeves, trying to hold that warm light inside them for another year.

I was sitting at a sidewalk table outside a saloon called Doc's, an old renovated brick tavern with high ceilings supported by dark stained beams, a mirrored oak-back bar, and enough ferns to start up a jungle. The front of the bar had glass doors that could be opened to the street. When the weather was fine you could sit outside, like I was, and watch the theater of bums and streetcorner preachers hitting up the Japanese tourists and avoiding the gray-suited lawyers coming back from the county courthouse. The bums knew the lawyers were lousy givers.

I drank my third slow beer straight from the bottle, washing the taste of work from my mouth. The beer was cold, and the sun was warm on my face. I was thirty-four years old, suddenly no longer broke, and still well enough not to make too many concessions to time. I had won my first jury trial in six months, my first big case in almost three years. And after three dry months I was falling off the wagon as gently as a child slides into its mother's arms.

A barmaid brought over my fourth beer. "You want some lunch? The kitchen's about to close till dinner."

"No, thanks," I replied.

"Must be pretty nice, taking the whole afternoon off to drink," she said.

"Nope," I answered. "It's hard work. Real Decadence requires Discipline. Dedication. And Self-Sacrifice." The barmaid gave me that long-suffering look that barmaids save for drunks and fools who think they're irresistible. I wasn't sure where I fit.

I let that afternoon slip away, time drifting lazily like a leaf in a river. The shadows in the green triangle of park across the street got longer, and the low light etched the streets in sharp relief, like a Hopper painting. The last of the late-season tourists stopped taking pictures, content to stroll and window-shop: heavyset men from Chicago or Dubuque and their equally solid wives, holding hands awkwardly, as if they hadn't held hands in years. The bums stopped panhandling and settled under the ornate glass and cast-iron pergola at the center of the square, content with their day's accumulation of loose change and sweet Tokay wine. Even the streetcorner preacher stopped calling down the wrath of God long enough to sit on a park bench, face upturned in communion with a stream of leaf-filtered light.

I watched idly as the man at the next table finished his beer and shuffled his papers and manila folders back into a thin brown-leather briefcase. He was doing what I should be doing, heading reluctantly back to his office. His calm, even face was as glum as any child who'd ever contemplated the first day of school. I caught his eye, and he grinned, then shrugged, and we were momentary conspirators, each of us ducking out of our ordinary lives. Then he slipped into his suit jacket, settled his tab, and stepped toward the street.

As he neared the street, an old Buick Electra, two-and-a-half tons of pure Detroit hog iron, pulled away from the far curb. It rolled slowly up the street and paused in front of the restaurant. Its windows were darkened with plastic film. The rear window facing the restaurant was rolled halfway down. A thin black tube poked out through the lowered car window. And suddenly, in the way you know the worst things, I knew what it was.

"Down," I shouted. "Down!" The man I later learned was Stephen Turner looked around, puzzled. He had only time to turn a little. By then the gunman had opened up.

The first shots went wide and shattered the restaurant windows behind me. I kicked over the cast-iron table in front of me and went down on the broken glass, clambering on all fours through the maze of overturned tables and tangled people, trying to reach Stephen Turner. An instinct from combat, I guess; you always bring the wounded and the dead back inside the line.

The gunman shot in a wide arc. Bullets slapped against the café tables and ricocheted off the brick sidewalk. Car tires squealed as the old Buick lurched away from the curb, leaving behind a cloud of blue greasy smoke and a sullen battlefield silence, a mixture of shock and fear and anger and pain.

Stephen Turner lay on his back in the gutter, his chest torn open. Blood ran from his chest and mouth and pooled thickly in the gutter. I didn't touch him. No need to. There was nothing that anyone could do for him again.

Beside me a man sobbed, a great heavy rasping sound. Sirens began to howl faintly in the distance. Finally the great barren wall of silence shattered like glass amid the sudden cacophony of people crying, screaming, shouting, trying to call for the cops and care for the injured and tend to the dead.

Within minutes the street looked like the Jewish quarter of Paris or the Green Line in Beirut, just another small random tragedy in the long, bloody course of the twentieth century. It was jammed with police cars and televison vans. Ambulances snaked slowly through the crowded block, their sirens wailing in frustration. Plainclothes cops stood around and whispered into radios while the uniforms blocked off the crime scene. Newspaper reporters in jeans and sneakers shouted at TV reporters in blue suits who combed their hair and waited for a chance to stand in front of the bullet-shattered facade of the restaurant. A crowd started to form at the barricades. A few decent people were crying. Some of the others had that look you see at auto races and wrestling shows. The look of blood sports, as old as the Romans.

I held a bloody bar-towel compress to the leg of a pretty barmaid. She was short and brown and smoothly round, face framed by short, straight brown hair, a portrait in earthtones. She wore one of those cocktail outfits, a tight black top and just enough skirt. She sat leaning against the building, knees up, sipping forty-dollar Martel cognac straight from the bottle. She flinched as I picked a few strands of ruined stocking away from the jagged wound in her thigh.

Her face was pale from the loss of blood, but she lit a cigarette anyway. She held the cigarette to my mouth, and I drew in smoke and blew it out gratefully. The cigarette, like my hands, was smeared with blood.

"Not too much longer," I said, trying to reassure her.

She smiled. Her teeth were small and white. "I think I'm going to be okay."

"I know you are."

"Really? You been shot before?" Her voice was sarcastic.

"Yes. In Vietnam."

"Oh." She hesitated. Then she said, softly, "I've never been this scared before. I was hit and knocked down, and I knew they were shooting. And I thought I was going to die. Only I didn't think of it that way. I just thought I'd never eat lasagna again, or drink too much wine, or make love."

She closed her eyes, and her face got whiter. I said, "That's a pretty normal way to feel. And when you're feeling better, you'll want to do everything at once, dance and laugh and party and make love all night."

She opened her eyes and smiled. She said, "Promise me you'll be there when I feel better."

I said, "Any time, love," just as the ambulance crew came and put on a pressure bandage and loaded her away. I heard that she was okay. But I never saw her again.

I lit another one of the barmaid's cigarettes and stood on the sidewalk smoking. A reporter I knew named Wilson rushed over, shaking with the adrenaline rush. She said excitedly, "Hey, Matt, talk to me, please. I've got questions." She paused. That's funny," she added, "I didn't know that you smoked."

I hadn't, in over a year. I took a hot, harsh drag and dropped the cigarette on the sidewalk and blew out the smoke. "Only when I get shot at," I replied.

CHAPTER 2

Four hours later I sat at the rear bar at Doc's, sullenly applying Scotch as a general anesthetic and waiting to get interviewed one more time by one of the dozen cops who still haunted the scene. The police had closed the street and boarded up the front of the bar, but the owner of Doc's, a fat radio announcer with the cheerful soul of a Borgia, kept the back door open and the booze flowing to a thirsty crowd of cops, gawkers, and almost-victims.

When Vincent Ahlberg walked through the back door of the joint, he had the kind of tired look you see in the faces of soldiers in old war photos. Bone-aching, grit-eyes, soul-weary tired. Ahlberg was a Seattle police lieutenant and the skipper of the homicide squad. He was an old-line cop with not much imagination but no illusions. Not tall, but broad and strong, he dressed well, courtesy of a rich almost–ex-wife. That night he looked old and shrunken inside a six-hundred-dollar London suit that had been hand-tailored but no longer seemed to fit. He and I were, and are, almost friends, a rare condition for cop and lawyer but not completely unheard of.

He pushed gently through the crowd, stopping here and there for a quick report from one of his men or one of the FBI crime-scene analysts who stood around in their black wing tips and J.C. Penney gray suits. After a while I caught his eye, and he nodded. He started over but was stopped by one of his sergeants, a large, pale, stupid man named Gooding. Gooding jerked a thumb in my direction, then pointed at a sheet of paper he held in his other hand. Vince nodded gravely, took the sheet, and joined me at the bar.

"H'lo, bartender," he said slowly. "Double Chivas, one rock. And whiskey or whatever for my friend here. Hello, Matthew. Shitty day, wasn't it?" His whiskey came, and he swallowed half of it. "I'm now officially off duty," he sighed.

"Good. What did Gooding want with me?"

"Gooding? Oh, the big fella. Just been detailed to me, and I'm already working on the paperwork to get rid of him." He swallowed the other half of his drink. "Wanted to arrest you."

"What'd you tell him?"

"I told him it was a good idea. Only thing is, they haven't made being a smart-mouthed shyster an indictable offense. Yet."

"He have any other charges?"

"He seemed upset that you used the term *motherfucker* five times in a witness statement. I think he's a lay preacher with the Nazarenes."

"Being shot at from a public street upsets me. Then again, so does he."

Ahlberg sighed and said, "Don't make fun of us cops, Matthew; we're having a bad day. Besides, you get enough of that kind of entertainment in court."

"Sorry."

"No problem. So you were here for the shooting?"

"Yeah. In my second-row seat, peacefully drinking lunch."

"Tell me about it. Slowly. I want to hear how it sounds."

So I told it again, trying to keep it straight despite the whiskey fuzzing my brain. Ahlberg interrupted occasionally, filling the story out. "We found the car," he said. "Dumped at the Marginal Way off-ramp. Must have had another car ready. No report from the lab yet, but it's going to be clean."

"Why?"

"Because this bastard is good."

When I finished, he said, "Was the shooter aiming at the guy in the street—Turner?—or was he spraying the crowd?"

"Don't know. Wait." I closed my eyes, concentrating. "He did spray the crowd, but Turner must have been the main target, because the car rolled up to the restaurant, like it had been parked down at the corner, waiting, just as Turner walked into the street."

Ahlberg nodded. "That makes sense. Could be just coincidence, but I doubt it."

"So, what was this all about?"

"Don't know yet. The pattern looks almost like a mob killing. Remember Crazy Joey Gallo, who got it eating pasta in New York? Except that Doc's doesn't serve Italian food. Maybe it was drugs."

"Or a political assassination."

He snorted. "This isn't Beirut. Political killings aren't one of the local pastimes. Baseball, football, the Sonics. Not shootings. It's bad for the quality-of-life image."

Nothing uses up alcohol like an argument. I ordered another round.

When we had tasted our drinks, I asked, "What about the victim, Turner?"

"Well, he's got a rich family. And he works for a computer company. Worked." He sipped his drink. "Three others wounded: the barmaid you looked after and a machine-tool salesman and his client, a tool wholesaler. All very respectable citizens. Which means the mayor is gonna jump on my ass from a considerable distance if we don't clear this one fast."

We both got quiet, staring into our whiskeys as if they had some answers. I hadn't been a prosecutor in some years, but I could still glibly trade theories of the shooting and compare box scores of the dead and wounded. And never think until I needed to that there was one family grieving and two others sweating out the long, hard hours by a hospital room.

We were blasted out of our gloom by the booming radio baritone of the bar owner. "Hey, shut the fuck up back there!" he yelled, each syllable clear, his vibrato ringing through the air. He turned up the volume on the bar-top TV, and we listened:

"BULLETIN. KSSJ TELEVISION HAS JUST LEARNED THAT A TER-RORIST GROUP CALLING ITSELF THE PACIFIC LIBERATION FAC-TION HAS CLAIMED RESPONSIBILTY FOR TODAY'S SHOOTING IN PIONEER SQUARE. AN UNNAMED SPOKESPERSON FOR THE GROUP TELEPHONED SEATTLE *TRIBUNE* COLUMNIST MARK SITWELL TO CLAIM CREDIT FOR THE ASSAULT. ONE MAN, STEPHEN TURNER

OF WEST HIGHLAND DRIVE, SEATTLE, DIED IN THE SHOOTING. THREE OTHERS WERE WOUNDED, ONE SERIOUSLY. VICTOR MIRAVCHEK, GENERAL MANAGER OF PACIFIC TOOLS, IS IN SERIOUS BUT STABLE CONDITION AT HARBORVIEW HOSPITAL. DETAILS AT ELEVEN.''

The television went back to a tampon commercial. Vince Ahlberg muttered ''son of a bitch'' and was gone, shoving his way through a quiet barroom crowd.

I drank for a while longer, but it wasn't any good. I kept thinking of Tu Do Street in Saigon, a main street for bars and cafés, sunny and noisy underneath the few shade palms. After thirty days in the bush I would grab a hot shower and head straight there for French champagne so cold it hurt. For a lot of us that street was like a vision of a better world. The VC figured that out and began hitting the street as often as they could. Most of us loved the street and never stopped going. But when you sat at a sidewalk table there, you always kept your eyes moving, wondering if the old man's bicycle was loaded with plastique or the flower girl carried a frag grenade in her basket. And you knew the world was a very fragile place.

CHAPTER 3

The pink phone slip said that a Mrs. Katherine Warden had called and wanted to discuss retaining me for a "personal legal matter," and would I drop by her home between one and three to discuss it. The message held the airy condescension of the rich or the crazy, and I could always use the money or the laugh.

It turned out to be rich. Mrs. Warden lived in the northwest part of town, along a shady residential road. On the east side of the road, away from Puget Sound, ordinary, comfortably large bungalows lined the street. On the west side loomed the waterfront houses of the wealthy—a street, a low stone wall, an acre of yard, and the better part of half-a-million dollars away.

The Warden house stood at the end of a quarter mile of flagstone driveway. It was an enormous gray shingled box with fifteen or twenty dormer windows at the roofline, like a Cape Cod cottage on steroids. It was topped at the roofline by a white-railed widow's walk big enough for a battalion of widows. Whaling having since gone out of style, the widows probably sipped gin and tonic while anxiously waiting for hubby's turbo Mercedes to heave to over the horizon.

I parked my battered, half-restored MG beside a marble stoop and stood before a pair of doors that would have admitted the L.A. Lakers and wondered what the hell I was getting into. I rang the bell. One door cracked open. A dark Latin face peered out.

"Señor?"

I shifted into rusty Spanish. "Señora Warden, por favor. Me llamo Riordan."

"Momento, señor." She turned away, and I heard the rattle of rapid-fire Spanish. Then a warm liquid contralto voice said, "Quite all right, Marta; I'll take care of it." The door opened wide, and a strong, heavy, but handsome woman dressed in bulky tweeds said, "Mr. Riordan? I'm Mrs. Carruthers, the housekeeper. Please follow me. Mrs. Warden is in the sunroom."

I followed her through an entrance hall bigger than my house, past dimly lit dayrooms that seemed covered by layers of abandonment. We walked up a wide oak staircase, its steps softened by an Oriental runner that must have used up four generations of Persians. Double doors at the top opened to a sunroom.

I hesitated in the doorway long enough to look the room over. Painted eggshell-white, it was flooded with light, even on this gray afternoon. At one end of the room low white sofas clustered around a fireplace; at the other, bookshelves were built into the walls. A carved cherry writing desk stood in front of the books. The marks of use—a scatter of papers on the desk, books marked with slips of paper and stacked on a shelf, an open stereo cabinet—kept the room from having that *Architectural Digest* look of sterile perfection. It was a good room, with the same sense of beauty within order that a Japanese garden has.

Katherine Warden stood on a narrow deck overlooking the water, staring at the cold gray-green waters of the sound and the low fog-shrouded islands in the distance. She was tall and slender and darkly blond, expensively dressed in leather jeans and a cashmere sweater. When she turned, I saw her face in three-quarter view. Her eyes were large and brown, not the blue I'd expected, and they were what you noticed even before the smooth elegance of her features. She had once, I thought, been merely pretty, but nearing forty her face had leaned and become beautiful.

The housekeeper, Mrs. Carruthers, stepped out to the deck and gently touched her arm, as if to lead her back into the room. The two of them spoke in low tones I couldn't hear, heads bowed together. Then Mrs. Carruthers stepped back into the room, leading the way, and said, "Mr. Riordan, this is Mrs. Warden." Katherine Warden nodded at me and gestured to the sofas near the fireplace.

We sat down and looked each other over for a long, awkward moment. Her eyes were red-rimmed and puffy, from tears or maybe alcohol. There was a kind of fragility in her face, a surface tension, as if her skin were made of very old glass and the sightest blow would fracture it.

She spoke quietly. "Three days ago my brother, Stephen Turner, was shot and killed. He had just left a restaurant down in the Pioneer Square district and was walking down a street when he was shot from a passing

car. The killer took his time and put four bullets in him."
Her voice was cold, clinical, exact, and dead.

Saying "I'm sorry" seemed inadequate. I said, "I was
there, at the same restaurant. I saw the shooting. I wish I
had some answers for you about it. But I don't."

She nodded, unsurprised. "I've spoken with the police,
Mr. Riordan. Nearly half-a-dozen times. They've given
me their reports, even some of the witness statements. It
doesn't amount to anything." She gestured irritably at the
scatter of official papers on the floor. "That's why I've
asked you to come here. I need to hear what happened."

I shook my head. "It's ugly and not worth telling, Mrs.
Warden, if you already know the facts." I had sat through
this scene too many times before, as a federal prosecutor.
Getting the victim's family ready for trial in a case when
murder couldn't be proved but racketeering or a civil rights
violation could be, you took the family through the grim
details of the death and tried not to hurt them too badly
when they asked you why their father or their brother was
killed. I always told the truth. I told them that their
father's car had been wired with a pipe bomb because he
had been extorting protection from the wrong set of already protected taverns or was saving his own ass on
trafficking charges by setting up a buy with the local
cocaine distributor. They always hated me for it, which
was unnecessary. I already hated myself for it.

"Please," she said. "I want to know what to do, for my
brother and myself. I'm not afraid. I'm one hell of a lot
tougher than you think."

There was no way to be kind and no way to argue. So I
told her about my sunny afternoon off that had been so full
of light and then suddenly of blood. When I was done

talking, she got up and poured squat crystal tumblers half-full of bourbon. I took mine and swallowed gratefully. She sipped at hers, oddly calm and detached.

"Tell me about yourself, Mr. Riordan. The people who told me about you were a little sketchy."

Every client is entitled to one silly question and one polite answer. More, if it looks like they can pay their bills. "There's not much to tell, Mrs. Warden. I was rasied up in western Montana, but went to school back east. I dropped out and got drafted. From the army I went to work as an investigator with the Justice Department in Washington. Finished college and a lot of law school at night and went back to work as a prosecutor in Boston. I tried corporate law for a few years in New York and didn't like it. Two years ago I moved back west and started my own practice."

"What kind of work do you do?"

"Mostly trial work, plaintiff's injury, and I get some criminal referrals from some of the big downtown firms that don't want to get their hands dirty. I'm afraid I wouldn't be much good at handling your brother's estate. I can refer you to some specialists in that sort of thing."

"That's not what I have in mind. Tell me, do you think the police will be able to find Stephen's killer?"

"I don't know," I said slowly. "It's had a lot of publicity. Your family and your money means enough politically so they won't just file it away. But it's not the sort of case they're good at. They've got no physical evidence, obvious suspects, or even a motive. Hell, they can't even be sure your brother was the target; maybe it really was just a crazy random terror shooting. If the cops can't find something soon, they might have to downplay it. I'm not saying they'd close it, but they might not be out beating the bushes and violating constitutional rights with their usual fervor.''

She nodded. ''I want to know who killed Stephen. And I want to know why. Will you find out for me, Mr. Riordan?''

I shook my head no. ''I'm not a private investigator, Mrs. Warden. I've been a Justice Department investigator, and I've directed some investigations as an attorney. But most of the things I worked on were tax cases or racketeering investigations. A lot of that work is tracing money from a criminal organization and following the paper trail through a legitimate company used to launder drug money or political money. It's more like accounting than anything else. The corporate investigations are pretty much the same. I've worked with numbers, Mrs. Warden. And with scared soft office managers, hoping to hang on to their pensions and praying that nobody checks the postage meter or the paper clip count. The kind of people who open fire with automatic weapons on a crowded restaurant are way out of my league.''

She leaned forward, face flushed. ''Riordan, I had two investigators in here yesterday, in their pastel suits and zircon pinky rings. Since I didn't need somebody skip-traced or spied on in bed, they couldn't help me. I had the corporate security firms come in, looking like Nixon's White House staff, all Southern Cal tans and cleft chins and sincere gray suits, and after all their double-talk about 'private public cooperation in ongoing police matters,' they couldn't help me.'' She stood up and walked to windows at the back of the room, then came back. ''Look, I don't care if all you can do is read police reports and push the cops and call press conferences to embarrass the mayor. I have to do something.'' She lowered her voice. ''Somebody killed Stephen for a reason. They went to time and trouble and expense. Damn it, find me the reason.''

''You may not like it, once you know.''

''What I like or don't like doesn't matter.'' Her hands made an irritable gesture of dismissal. She sat down and leaned back against the sofa, suddenly spent.

''Okay,'' I heard myself saying. ''Tell me about your brother.''

CHAPTER 4

A very smart cop once told me that a murder investigation should always begin with the victim. Ninety percent of the time, he said, the victim knows the killer, or at least knows why he's being done in. The killing cuts the complex web of the victim's social connections. Follow those connections and you can reconstruct the reason for the killing, and that will identify the killer.

Besides that, he said, swallowing the last of his beer and heading for the door, most of the time you don't have the faintest fucking idea of where else to start.

So I started with Stephen Turner.

The newspapers had said that he was thirty-five years old. He had a degree in math and designed computer software for a small local company called macroprocess— all small letters—that sold software and computer services. No wife, no children. He had once been a prominent student radical at the University of Washington. He wasn't in politics anymore, but he gave a lot of money to charities that actually fed people instead of producing TV shows. He spent a lot of nights working for a nuclear freeze. Not a bad idea. One nuclear bomb can ruin your whole day.

That was it. Just enough to fill the three paragraphs between the wire service lead and the reporter's attempt to turn three "no comments" and a minor leak into an educated guess about the progress of the police investigation.

Katherine Warden had added a little more. The next day we sat out on her deck and watched the sun break through the clouds before it slipped down behind the newly white peaks of the Olympic range, drinking local ale and talking about her brother the way you talk about the newly dead, a mixture of laughter and pain and sharp nostalgia, like when you think about a summer love who broke your heart.

The Turner family had started getting rich from nineteenth-century timber and railroad interests and twentieth-century oil and steel. Katherine Warden's father, Hamilton Turner, had shifted the family holdings into real estate and telecommunications, just in time for the 1970s boom in those areas to make the family very well-off indeed. They now owned sizable chunks of Seattle and San Francisco, some TV stations, and enough banks and real estate to regard the state of Idaho as an asset, still being leased but with an option to purchase.

Stephen Turner had fit into this background of comfortable, anonymous power and wealth about as well as Jerry Falwell would at the Coyote Hookers' Ball.

"He wasn't a rebellious kid, exactly," Katherine Warden said. "More determined. Self-rightous. At fifteen he hitchhiked around the country. At sixteen he denounced us all as corrupt and debauched. We're a Catholic family, so

Steve joined the Franciscans for a while. Later he turned onto the Church all the fury he had let loose on us." She paused and sipped her beer. "I think that's why he liked mathematics so much. Pure and absolute. No suffering, no gray areas, not like people at all. Or maybe he thought it was the highest form of human art, I don't know."

"The newspapers all said he was active in the sixties student movement, antiwar activities."

"He lived for the movement for a long time. He joined SDS, Students for a Democratic Society, at nineteen. He was in Chicago in 1968, with Abbie Hoffman and Tom Hayden and all the rest. I was at home with my parents and we watched on TV while he got clubbed down outside McCormick Place."

"I take it your parents did not approve."

"Oh, God, no. He and Dad used to shout at each other for hours."

She laughed. "Once he called Mother, said he was bringing a very nice girl home for dinner. Would Mother mind? Mother was thrilled, a sign of normality at last. She set the table with the silver, brought in an extra servant, thought up about six courses. Steve wore a jacket and tie. The girl had on a dress, makeup, and even stockings. They ate and drank and chatted, very polite. After dinner and brandy, Steve told us who she was. Elizabeth Doheny."

"A very prominent Weatherperson. Now serving time for bank robbery."

"Steve asked Dad how he liked becoming an accessory to interstate flight from prosecution. Said it was the first time the crime had been committed with caviar."

Katherine laughed again and looked far away. I thought I knew a little bit of what she was going through. All of

21

her immediate family was dead. So was mine. When you are the last one left, you lose some sense of restraint on your life. There is no one left who can judge you, whose judgment you cannot completely escape.

Katherine said that in 1971 Turner and eight others had been indicted on state charges of criminal conspiracy. The press had called them the Northwest Nine. They were supposed to be the masterminds behind a series of demonstrations and bombings at federal courthouses and power stations throughout Washington and Oregon.

After they were acquitted, Turner had disappeared into the Weather Underground, the hardened fringe of the sixties movement. Six months later he reappeared, disillusioned by the turn to bank robbery and kidnapping as a form of political expression. He finished his degree and got a California teaching certificate. He taught school in the Oakland ghetto for six years. Laid off in a 1981 budget cutback, he came back to Seattle to find work. Eventually he got a job writing computer software for the local Seattle firm that became macroprocess.

Katherine said that her memories of the years after Steve had come home to Seattle seemed blurred together in her mind. They had been together for the death of their parents. He had spent dozens of sleepless nights with her after her husband and infant daughter had died in a sliding crash on snowbound Interstate 90, standing the suicide watch, hiding the pills and the booze and the razor blades until he had presuaded her to live again. They had grown close, each pulling the comfort of their settled ways around them like an old worn blanket. Finally even that comfort had been ripped away.

*   *   *

Over the next few days I dug out all the records I could find on Stephen Turner, just the way they teach you to do it in a mail-order detective course. I subpoenaed his driving records from the Department of Licensing and found out that he had been cited for failure to signal a lane change on Interstate 5 at two in the morning on June 6, 1980. The City of Seattle business department had never heard of him. His credit bureau report noted that he paid his bills on time—unusual for a millionaire—and contained a completely illegal notation on his politics. A short chat with the credit bureau manager about the Fair Credit Reporting Act got me a copy of the credit report and a list of Turner's charge account numbers. I checked his accounts. If he was still buying into the revolution, he wasn't putting it on his American Express card.

I called three cops, a taxi driver, a pimp, and the only drug dealer I knew with standards—he wouldn't sell to anybody under the age of fourteen unless they paid full retail price. I called two hookers, one cheap, one expensive, and three gay clients. None of them had ever heard of him.

Katherine gave me the names of three women Turner had recently dated. One was a stunning blond marketing specialist who wore more expensive suits than I did in court and structured her life into twenty-minute blocks. She said I could have two blocks between her last appointment and her aerobics class. She told me it just could never have worked out between them, you know, commitment was impossible to work into her goal structure. After the blonde I needed three drinks to deal with number two, the former roller disco queen of Snohomish County, who said Steve had been just a short-term thing. The third was a pale slender redheaded schoolteacher who had been to the funeral and missed Steve dreadfully, they had become *such friends,* and who offered to ball me if I was ever in the neighborhood. At least he had eclectic taste. All three of them were very sorry he was dead and had no idea who could have done such a terrible thing.

Turner lived in an old but still elegant brick eight-plex walk-up on the south shoulder of Queen Anne Hill. I hiked up to the top floor and fumbled with Katherine's keys in front of the door. The police had come and gone again. The remnants of a department seal were still taped to the wooden door frame.

I had thought that Turner might still live in the nostalgic slop of the sixties. Wrong again. His small apartment was sparsely furnished. A hard-looking Danish wool sofa faced a picture window that overlooked most of the city and part of Elliot Bay. A ceiling-high bookshelf filled one wall; a refinished oak library-table was pushed against the other. The tabletop was cleared away, and the books on the shelf were lined up with military precision. There was no dust in the corners. It was the home of someone who had lived alone for a long time and had gotten good at it.

The bedroom was much the same. Turner had slept on a platform bed pushed into one corner. A portable TV stood staring on top of a single chest of drawers, electronic Valium available at the touch of a switch.

In the kitchen most of the food had rotted, but I found a cold six-pack of Olympia beer tucked away in the icebox. I took a can out and sipped it while I settled down to search.

Searching a house is seldom dull. To most people, a

home is the last refuge from the prying eyes of a society that always seems to be demanding that they be something they are not. If they have a second life—sex, drugs, crazed urges for pistachio and pedophilia, whatever—they keep it at home. When I was a kid I worked summers for an uncle at his northern Wisconsin resort. One of the local leaders in the tourist and timber county was a Methodist-Episcopal bishop named Wintergreen. He was a big man, square-shouldered, with a strong, blunt, kindly face and flowing white hair. He lived in a bit white cottage on the shore of the Rhinelander River and took devoted care of his invalid wife. He would go out to the tourist campgrounds and preach sermons so sweet that Chicago steelworkers who lived for their two fishing weeks a year would give up Sunday mornings on the lake to hear him. My last summer there, he died of a heart attack. When they went to clear out his house and close his estate, they found enough pornographic books and gadgetry to franchise a whorehouse chain, and, rumor had it, photos of the bishop with more than a few of the tourist wives. Nothing was proved, but the county sheriff retired to Florida that winter.

If Turner had such a life, I wasn't finding it.

I found a missing sock pushed into the corner of the closet. I found the hole where the mice came in, under the kitchen sink, the end of their own Ho Chi Minh trail that began in the cellar, four floors below. I found a forgotten phone bill and a misplaced ticket to the Seattle Repertory Theater. And just when I began to despair that Turner wasn't an ordinary human being, I found his stash.

It was taped up underneath the carved crown molding that trimmed his antique bookshelf, wrapped in a long tube of dark shiny green plastic. Low marks for ingenuity, I thought as I unwrapped it. The green plastic bag contained about an ounce of California sinsemilla, the Château Mouton-Rothschild of marijuana, and better than half a pound of cocaine.

The coke bothered me. It is a drug with powerful attractions for people who work mostly with their minds. You feel sharper, faster, sexier, more powerful, more controlled. A couple of years ago, fresh out of the government and making more money in New York law than I'd thought existed, I'd gotten some very decent cocaine from a record producer as a private bonus for working out a successful contract. Very mellow, I thought; just do a few lines with friends before a party. I blew most of it the first weekend. Three weeks and thirty-five-hundred dollars later, I decided that anything that much fun really *ought* to be illegal.

The amount bothered me even more. A gram and a half, street-cut, will keep two real estate agents obnoxious all night. When you weigh it in ounces, it is night-moves time, man, that electric-smoky-lowlife-latenight-raunch. Turner could easily afford it, but it seemed inconsistent with his intensely religious background and his devotion to political causes. I rewrapped the package and carefully taped it back into place, wondering why the cops hadn't spotted it. It was so obvious a hiding place, maybe they planted it themselves.

I worked my way down the bookcase, checking books at random for anything slipped between the pages. Turner's literary taste ran to religious and policital philosophy—Plato, Aquinas, Marx, Trotsky, Rousseau—and to Russian novelists so somber they made Turgenev seen like a stand-up comic.

On the bottom shelf I found a pair of thick black three-ring notebooks filled with carefully indexed photocopies of newspaper clippings. They were trial publicity books, prepared by Turner's lawyers for the conspiracy trial back in 1971. Trial lawyers prepare them in important, expensive cases so they can understand what prospective jurors have read in the press and what biases they may have formed. Turner apparently kept them as a sort of ironic souvenir.

I sat down on Turner's sofa with a fresh beer and, while the city lights below me switched on like a sweeping tide of stars, began to read.

CHAPTER 5

The receptionist at the suburban offices of macroprocess sat behind a white plastic desk sterile enough to do surgery on. I stood and waited while she played a computerized telephone switchboard that glowed and buzzed and magically commanded MBAs in three-piece suits and computer nerds in T-shirts and jeans to scurry around the gray and pastel offices. While I waited, I looked at the receptionist. She had a full but not heavy figure and still had a dark summer tan beneath an elegant cream silk dress. Her blond hair looked real and fell in soft natural waves, the kind that takes hours of effort or a Ph.D. hairdresser. She was the kind of woman who works an ordinary job but lunches at French restaurants with pro basketball players and sails with department store heirs. Not in my league.

I gave her my name, and she told me that Thomas Darwin, the company president, wasn't in but that he knew I was working on the Turner case and he wanted to help. I could find him at home and should stop there by noon. And then she was on to the next call, her voice as smooth and bright and hard as a stone polished by running water.

Darwin lived on Capitol Hill, an old and once-again elegant neighborhood above downtown Seattle. His flat was the penthouse apartment of a whimsical, turreted brick building on the edge of Volunteer Park. It had been built in the 1920s by a man named Anhalt, a self-taught architect who had apparently been inspired by tales of Camelot. Anhalt had built this castle on a small knoll above the street. It floated above its neighbors on a sea of leafy green trees just barely touched by the first color of the fall. Old Anhalt may have been mad, but his buildings always made me feel like sir Gawain instead of a bit player in a Bauhaus nightmare.

The man who met me in the hall said he was Tom Darwin and shook my hand. "I'm just about to put on another pot of coffee; want some?" he asked. I said yes and followed him into his kitchen.

Darwin was tall but not big, rather narrow-shouldered and soft-looking, a grown-up version of the kid who was always a disappointment to the basketball coach. He was thirty-five or forty. His beard was heavy but closely trimmed. He wore horn-rimmed glasses, not the new trendy kind but the old-fashioned heavy ones. They constantly threatened to slide off his nose.

"I like your building," I said.

"I've always loved it, since the first time I saw it as a kid," he replied.

"You must have read 'Prince Valiant' in the comics."

"Sure did. Which one of the knights did you want to be?"

"Galahad, I guess."

"Why?"

"I'm not sure. After I was twelve, I guess I figured he was getting it on with Aleta while Prince Val was off on the Crusades."

He laughed as he put the pot of fresh coffee and two heavy cups on a tray, then carried it back to the room that served as a study. Papers and computer runs cascaded onto the floor around a large personal computer setup. We settled into low brown armchairs to talk.

"I'm a lousy company president," he said cheerfully, loading cream and sugar into his coffee. "I've got a business manager, a Stanford MBA. He's a good guy, but he just purely drives me crazy. Meetings, appointments, conference calls. Everything's urgent. He even sends me memos he calls 'actiongrams.' No shit." He shook his head and laughed. "So, I take two mornings a week just to stay home and get some work done."

"What kind of work do you do?"

"Oh, software design and development, mostly. We have a half-dozen big-selling programs for personal computers. But we also do custom programming for companies with a big universe of data to shove around, like banks or oil companies. Some real challenges there." He grinned. "I try to hog some of that work for myself."

"When did you get to know Steve?" I asked.

Darwin paused and looked thoughtful. "Before we get into that—and hey, I don't want to be rude—but I don't understand what you're dong in all this. I've talked to the cops, and so has half the company. What're you doing that they're not?"

"Not much, probably," I admitted. "I'm a lawyer.

Katherine Warden, Stephen's sister, hired me to follow up on the police investigation, clear up the unexplored areas, push a little. She knows that there are limits on what I can do. But if she wants to try, I think she's got the right.''

"And it's a buck for you," he said flatly.

"Yes. But not a dishonest one."

"I suppose not." He sounded unsure. "We want to do everything we can to find Steve's killer. We kept a copy of all our employees' statements to the police, and you can have a copy."

"And I'll take them, with thanks. How long have you known Turner?" I persisted.

When he answered, there was a hint of annoyance in his voice, as if he were not used to answering questions. "Let's see. I met Steve in 1981, just after he'd moved back to Seattle. He came to work for us about a month later."

"What did he do?"

"Oh, marketing mostly. He got our first PC program into the stores just by ragging the retailers half to death. But he also did some of the custom programming, and designed educational programs. Steve knew computers pretty well; he started with it as a hobby back in the mid-seventies. That's the good thing about this line of work: you don't need a degree; you just learn and then do what you want."

"Was he working on anything special in the last year or so?"

"No, just the educational software. Steve worked on that stuff because he believed in it. You know, he was a teacher for a while, and the idea of these programs is to have the computers teach the rote stuff—vocabulary, multiplication tables—and free up the teacher to provide real attention. It may sell very well." He added ironically, "But I don't think anyone would shoot him because of a new reading program."

"Anything else you can think of?"

"No. Oh, he'd gotten more politically active in Target/zero, the Seattle antinuclear group, worked on that a lot of the time, both in Seattle and in the Bremerton area, at the submarine base."

"His politics bother you?"

"Not that way. Nuclear war is likely to be bad for business. I'd heard that he was a student radical once, but, hell, most of us were once."

Darwin fidgeted in his chair, obviously anxious to get back to work. "So, what else can we do for you, Mr. Riordan?"

"Two things. I'd like to see Turner's personal files, his desk files. And I'd like to talk to a couple of people on your staff, the ones who worked closely with him." It never hurts to ask.

Darwin was wearing a frown I could see right through his beard. "I don't think so," he said slowly. "It could be very disturbing to the other folks in the company. And those files would have a lot of sensitive stuff in them, trade secrets. There's piracy all over the software business."

"Maybe I'll just tag along with the cops on their next visit," I said.

Darwin started to cloud over with anger, then thought better of it. "Look, Riordan, this thing is a real tragedy. But I don't see what it has to do with macroprocess. The company's solvent and growing like mad. I'm not greedy; most of the staff has a piece of the equity, and they're going to do damn well when we go public. Nobody would want to hurt the company and screw that up. I know about the terrorist group claiming responsibility. I think he was killed by a bunch of political maniacs. But even that wouldn't involve macroprocess. We don't do any military-type work or any 1984–type stuff. I just don't see us as a target."

It was time to go. I stood up and said, "I hope you're right. Thanks for the time."

He stood up to show me out. "No problem. If you feel you really do need more information from us, let's kick it around. Give my lawyer, Arthur McAdams a call anytime."

That was not much of an offer. Trying to pull information out of a corporate lawyer with anything less than a show-cause contempt order is just so much polite beating-off. I could see good reasons for Darwin's caution. If the company was going to go public and sell stock, putting the unsolved murder of a senior employee into the offering statement wasn't going to do wonders for the price. But the door had shut just a little too quickly and a little too tight.

Darwin walked me out, back through a designer living room that looked like an expensive hotel lobby, all low pastel parsons sofas and little glass tables. I would have guessed that he spent no time there at all except for the portrait that was hung over the fireplace. It was a standard sort of oil of a young woman wearing a Mexican blouse. Her light-brown hair was very long, and the artist had almost but not quite captured the sense of wind blowing through it. The woman had large light eyes that were very wide and very innocent, a look that I had not seen for a very long time. I thought she was very beautiful and said so to Darwin.

"Yes, she was," he said woodenly.

"First loves die hard," I said.

It was an inspired awful guess. He showed me to the door and didn't say anything at all. I felt a lot less like Sir Gawain by the time I hit the street.

It was nearing noon when I left Thomas Darwin, and I had a motion to argue in Superior Court on a three-o'clock setting, so I stopped at the Pike Place Public Market and bought an apple and a bottle of beer and headed back to my office.

My office was at 319-½ South Occidental, in Pioneer Square. It was a four-story brick walk-up. The building was owned by a dentist who had renovated it as a retirement project. He had sandblasted the brick and refinished the oak floors and put in skylights and potted palms. But his timing was bad. High interest rates had depressed the market, and as the dentist lowered his rents and went back to pulling teeth, the regular citizens came back. The Quik-Serv Bail Bonds Company, Mary Ellen's Secretarial School, and Asian Delights Escort Service. And me.

I settled in at my desk to read the other side's brief. It was four times too long, and the style could have put me to sleep even with four tabs of methamphetamine in my blood. But I plugged away at it and sipped my beer and enjoyed the luxury of an empty building's lunchtime silence.

The man drifted in so quietly that I sensed him—a faint stirring on the air—before I heard him.

"Mr. Riordan?" he asked softly.

I looked at up him over a volume of *Washington Reports*. He was tall and slender, dark-skinned from a trace of Indian blood or just a deep-water tan. His eyes were set like two dark stones in a face of lines and angles. He was the sort of man who could lower the temperature of a room just by walking in.

"That's right," I finally said. "So, what can the lawyer do for you today?"

"Just a few minutes of your time." His speech was unaccented but formal, almost Castilian in cadence. "Perhaps you might enjoy a walk. It is a very fine early autumn day."

"I think I would. But only if I know your name."

He hesitated. Not from shyness. Perhaps from a working knowledge of electronic surveillance equipment. Then he said, "Cruz. Henry Cruz."

I chewed that one over as I followed him out of my building. Henry Cruz was a sort of success story. Five or six years back the City of Tacoma, Seattle's gritty, aging little industrial neighbor, had exploded into a crime war over splitting the take from the wide open prostitution and drug rackets. After a dozen cases of arson and a half-dozen shootings, the Pierce County government and the United States Attorney cracked down. Three corruption trials had sent the gang leaders, a dozen politicians, the sheriff, and four county detectives to federal prison. The three or four county pols not on the take took credit for the cleanup.

But no town with two naval shipyards and an army base is going to stay clean very long. There is just too much loose money rolling in each month, steady as a river.

Henry Cruz walked into the vacuum. The rumor was that he had been a fixer in the San Jose mob in California, spreading the cash out to Santa Clara county bureaucrats when a zoning approval or a health-code check was needed. He came to Tacoma a few months after the trials had cleared out the old mob. He reorganized the massage parlors and strip joints, branching out into numbers and loan-sharking. Within two years Tacoma was quiet, organized, and, if you knew where to look, more wide open than ever. And it was a mob town. Not big league, just the minors, the mob's version of the Pacific Coast League with San Jose, Eureka, Santa Cruz and Oakland. Henry Cruz owned the franchise.

Cruz led me to a midnight-blue Cadillac limousine parked in the alley behind my building. It gleamed against the tired mud-colored brick like a hooker in an unemployment line. The driver was a strong dark man of perhaps twenty-five. He opened the doors wordlessly, moving with a quick, smooth athletic grace not often seen in men his size. I was going to be very careful not to antagonize him.

We rode in silence up to Volunteer Park. The limousine stopped at the brick water-tower, and Cruz and I walked among the flower beds that were still alive with late-season blooms.

"I enjoy coming here," he said quietly. "A very peaceful place, don't you agree?"

"I do. But I'm curious, Mr. Cruz. From what I hear you just about run Pierce County. That's not a profession that involves making house calls."

"I often find, Mr. Riordan, that I can solve a small problem just as it is starting by giving it my personal attention. This saves me considerable difficulty at later times."

"What sort of problem am I? Besides small."

"I don't know yet. I am told that you are, once committed, a very determined man. You have recently begun investigating the death of a man named Stephen Turner. I understand that you represent his family in this. Ordinarily that would be commendable. But for reasons of my own I must ask you to stop."

"I really don't know what you're talking about."

"Please, we should not waste our time this way. If you wish to speak hypothetically, we may. It is my advice that if you are involved in this matter, you should withdraw. If you do, I will see to it that you are compensated for any loss. It is also likely that you will receive a substantial amount of new legal business."

Cruz delivered a bribe with as much class as anyone I'd seen lately. I almost felt bad telling him no. He didn't seem surprised.

"In my view, you are being unwise," he said. "Perhaps very unwise."

"And the next time I get told it won't be gently. What I don't understand, Mr. Cruz, is why you want me to get out of it. Turner got killed in a very messy and very public way. There's going to be all kinds of pressure from the press and the politicians on the cops. They can't just this case drop."

He said, "The police would behave in ways I can predict. But you are an unknown. I did not kill Turner, and I did not order him killed. If I had, I would have chosen other methods." He smiled slightly, a cold, feral smile. "But, as I said, the reasons are my own."

"And if I ignore your advice, Mr. Cruz?"

"I will have to insist. But I am a patient man. You may receive an occasional reminder."

There was nothing left to say. We rode back downtown in silence. When I got out of the car, I saw Cruz's driver watching me carefully. So that he would know me again.

CHAPTER 6

The Turner murder slipped off the front pages as the story slowly suffocated for lack of news. The Seattle police had just about run out of creative ways to admit that they didn't know anything. Now it was just a "sensitive ongoing investigation," which, freely translated from cop talk, means "we don't know what the fuck is going on."

The FBI was not doing much better. The FBI has had a warm place in its heart for domestic political crimes ever since the good old days with J. Edgar, and recently terrorists had replaced Commies under the bed on their list of bad guys. But they were not making much progress. Vince Ahlberg had sent me a copy of their reports. The Bureau had set to work with its usual anal retentive efficiency, sifting the physical evidence, making computer searches through their Crime Information Center, checking on the whereabouts of retired radicals from the sixties, and probably tapping the telephone of anyone who ever voted for McGovern.

Their internal reports said no more than what they had told the papers. The Liberation Faction was not a "known terrorist organization." The Bureau "knew of no connection" between the Faction and the Armed Resistance Movement, a California group that had bombed an Officers' Club at the San Francisco Presidio the month before. After the first short phone call there hadn't been any other contact from the group. The Bureau didn't know whether they wanted to SAVE THE WHALES, FREE HUEY, OR STOP THE GENOCIDE IN (CENTRAL AMERICA? SOUTH AFRICA? SANDUSKY, OHIO?).

But one of the FBI agents, a man named Wheeler, said a very perceptive and very scary thing to Mark Sitwell, the columnist who had received the original call from the terrorists. Wheeler said:

"This isn't like anything we've had in the past here. In the 1960s and '70s we had some bombings by people who were usually very careful not to kill. If this was a terrorist action, it's more like the kind of random killing done by the Japanese Red Army or the PLO. In the Middle East, they figure that any Jew, any bystander, is guilty just because they are there."

With that grim thought from the morning paper, I took Turner's dusty press clipping notebooks out of my briefcase and set them on my desk. I couldn't figure out why he had kept them. People keep souvenirs of weddings. Family trips. Senior proms. Not when they get indicted on conspiracy charges.

But Turner's history and maybe his whole life had been tied up in those years of anger. Now he had been killed by what seemed like a twisted outbreak of the same nihilist rage. It was worth another look.

*　　*　　*

In the late 1960s and early 1970s the Pacific Northwest, like other parts of the country, staggered through a series of antiwar demonstrations and summertime riots. True to the region's radical heritage, the peaceful protests were punctuated by a series of well-executed bombings that targeted the region's more visible symbols of power and wealth: courthouses, banks, army depots, and powerlines. The bombings were the work of several different groups with different motives, ranging from extortion to anarchy. Many of the bombers had vague notions about setting free a proletariat that was pulling down twelve-fifty an hour at the aircraft plants and would have cheerfully lynched any Marxist they could get their hands on. It was lousy politics but much better romance, and the bombers cultivated the desperado image, reaching out to strike a target and then melting away into the farming valleys and high meadows of the Cascade Range.

Stephen Turner had been part of a loose collective of radical student leaders at the University of Washington. The group had started out in the mid-sixties as an outpost of earnest middle-class student liberalism, but by 1970, the collective had ties with the Weather Underground and political prisoners' groups up and down the West Coast. After Nixon's bombing of Cambodia, they were part of a violent demonstration that shut down the King County courthouse and trashed most of the city's financial district. The local cops and the National Guard responded with rubber bullets, water cannons, and mass arrests. The South American sounds of jackboots and rifle fire could be heard faintly on the air.

In late July of 1971, two electric power substations were

blown up in mountainous east King County. Most of Seattle was blacked out. A lineman was injured in the blast.

The county prosecutor at the time, Warren Hartlett, saw the bombing as an opportunity to break the student leadership and, not coincidentally, ride into the governor's chair. A county sheriff's informer claimed to have seen four of the leaders, including Turner, in a Fall City tavern near the power stations a week before the explosion. That kind of evidence is so thin that when you turn it sideways it disappears, but it was enough for Hartlett. In King County, the prosecutor doesn't have to go before the grand jury. For the next two weeks Hartlett handed out conspiracy indictments like they were free passes to the county fair.

By the time he got done there were nine of them, all students at the University of Washington, all active in SDS or the Black Students Union. Eight were white, one black. A county cop told me later that Hartlett would never have indicted the black kid except that he thought a jury would need to see a spade with a gun and a dashiki before they'd convict. All nine were smart. Most were middle-class. They probably never thought of themselves as a group, but after the indictments came down the press started calling them the Northwest Nine and the label hung on like mud at election time.

I looked hard at their faces, old photographs on yellowing newsprint. I knew better than to think I could look into a picture and see into someone's character, but I was transfixed.

They looked different from the people and I knew now, the way that the Russians or the French look different from Americans. Their faces were young, less polished and sleek than those I saw on the street. Their expressions were a mix of arrogance and innocence. Like fanatics. Or saints.

George Warren Shields, then and now, was affable and relaxed, oozing with the easy assurance that is the birthmark of the small-town rich. He was stocky, thick-lipped, and sensual; the rumor was that he had stayed home from many demonstrations to bed the girl friends of more zealous colleagues. He was not especially bright, but on a speaker's platform he was transformed and became compelling, charismatic, even daring. He had long since dropped out of radical politics. He practiced law in Seattle and won a State Senate seat as a conservative republican after a public recantation of his youthful politics. He was now actively running for Congress.

Deborah Greene was the philosopher-queen of Northwest radical politics during the 1960s. The daughter of two University of California professors, she had started as a doctrinaire Marxist, became a Maoist, then a number of increasingly silly things. She had stayed with revolutionary politics longer than any of the others. Emerging from the Weather Underground in Montreal n 1974, she studied literature at McGill University, taking a degree in 1976. She now taught women's literature and history at the University of British Columbia.

Mustafa Kemal, also known as Howard Franklin Rollins, Jr., was the only black member of the Nine. Once a Baptist divinity student, he had converted to the Black Muslim faith. He had been the link between black and white student groups. Now he ran a social service agency in the central district.

Danny Schoen had liked to pass himself off as a

streetcorner stud, a guerrilla fighter who could make an army out of the greaser kids who hung around the university area bars and clubs. His newspaper photos showed a half-tough kid with a weak face and long blond hair slicked back into a ducktail. Since the conspiracy trial, he had been busted twice for drug-dealing and had done a three-year stretch in the late seventies. A five-minute phone call told me that he was still dealing, mostly coke, out of a nightclub he owned in South Tacoma.

Diane Olmstead and Kyle Parman had been bit players picked up in the sweep. Diane Olmstead had been George Shields's longtime girl friend, something of a radical groupie. A tall blonde with patrician good looks, she had long since retreated to the safe comfort of her family and its money.

Kyle Parman was also at the fringes, but in a different way. He was an ex-con with a long juvenile record who had finally drawn time for assault on a cop during the bust of a chop shop operation. He had gone to the university on an early-release parole and discovered that his brain was stronger than his back, taking a degree in philosophy. He was older and more street-smart than the others, and they thought he was James Dean, the laid-back working-class hero. Now he ran an auto repair shop in Ballard called Spinoza Auto Repair.

Two others were dead. Blake Riddell and Janice Ivie had been killed in 1975 when their car rolled off Highway 101 a few miles south of Mendocino.

The government's case hadn't held up worth a damn. Hartlett had planned a carefully staged show trial that would position him politically even if he couldn't prove the charges. What he'd bought was a circus. The Nine had been represented by a legal team led by Edwin Kelleher, still one of Seattle's best lawyers. A graying ex-Marine, Kelleher had destroyed the government's informants with his meticulously researched cross-examination. He drew out each of the informers' past convictions, each dollar they'd been paid, each promise the prosecutor had made to get the testimony. Like Watergate, each revelation built upon all the earlier ones until lies and the truth looked and sounded and felt the same. It was anticlimactic when the jury found them not guilty. Even as the trial was ending, the war was winding down and the fires of protest had begun to die out.

I stretched and paced around my office. These were nine unremarkable people who had been connected by accident. The radical sixties were ancient history, washed out by the wave of self-indulgent good times, the mad urge everybody had in the 1970s to get theirs before all the good stuff was gone. It was a long shot to connect Turner's death to a past that was so remote it should be in a museum. But I couldn't quite believe that there were no links between the old violence and the new. Turner might have kept his connections with the few remaining radical groups and exposed some new, deadly purpose. Hell, I'd lived through times that rehabilitated Richard Nixon and produced the Symbionese Liberation Army. I thought anything was possible. Besides, following up on crazy ideas was the one sensible thing I could do in this case before I gave it up and told Katherine Warden to stop wasting her money, pack up her grief, and take it a good long way away.

I called up Vince Ahlberg. He wasn't at his desk, and the cop switchboard played Muzak while they looked for him. They do that in Seattle. Someday they'll play "Strangers in the Night'' to a rape victim, and I will personally sue them for one trillion dollars.

"I hear you've taken up private gumshoeing," he said with a dry chuckle in his voice.

"I get the feeling I was set up in the business by a prominent local law-enforcement officer."

"Well, yeah, that's probably what happened. Look, all kidding aside, there are very few private investigators in this town I trust. I know you won't fuck up the police work or start calling stupid press conferences, and, well, you might even come up with something we overlooked. If it costs her some bucks, hell, she can afford it. What are you up to, anyway?"

"I've just read all that paper you sent me and talked to a few people. You've got nothing, so far."

"Damn it, Matthew, I know that. And I know the mayor will curl up in Mrs. Warden's lap and then come down here and start discussing my early retirement if you put her up to it. That still isn't going to solve the case."

"I know. I'm going to stay out of your way. For a while. I'm going to talk to some of the people who were tried with Turner on the bombing case back in '71."

"What the hell for? The Bureau's already talked to most of them. They haven't seen one another in years."

"No good reason. Suspicion."

"Maybe paranoia. But at least it'll keep you out of the way," he said smugly.

"There's something I want from you," I said.

"What's that?"

"I want the Seattle Police Intelligence Unit files on the student demonstrations in the sixties and seventies. I know that one set of files was kept even after the city council

shut down the Intelligence Unit. Wade Walker told me."
Walker was a lawyer I knew who had sued the city some
years before for police harassment.

"No. That's crazy. It's got nothing to do with Turner's
death."

"I want them. If you need heat from the top to turn
them loose, that can be arranged."

"Fuck you," he snapped. The line went dead in my ear.

Yelling into a dead phone is worse than useless. I put
the phone down and flexed my hand a few times to loosen
it. Then I went and packed a bag and went down to the
garage for my car and the drive to Victoria.

CHAPTER 7

The Department of English Literature at the University of British Columbia was housed in one of those cantilevered steel, glass, and concrete buildings that looks like an airline terminal trying to do the standing long jump. The English Department office had concrete walls and floors painted gray and blue. Two deep-set small windows grudgingly admitted a little cloudy light. A small fig tree that looked like it needed chemotherapy drooped listlessly in one corner.

A friendly looking matron of fifty or so sat at a reception desk. She had iron-gray hair and a dotty smile and looked like she had mothered generations of neurotic undergraduates. She said, "Can I help you?"

"I suppose it's a little late to be registering for English 101," I replied.

"Yes, about two weeks. In your case, fifteen years," she said, laughing merrily.

"I was afraid of that. Actually, I'm here to see Professor Greene. I was told she'd be available after four. My name's Riordan."

"I'll see what I can do, Mr. Riordan. Have a chair, please."

I sat down on a thin, hard chair and picked up a literary journal. The lead article was about the fate of the Western Canadian novel. I had never read a Western Canadian novel and from the way the article talked about them I hadn't missed much.

Minutes crawled by silently. A little sunlight broke into the room, and I watched dust motes dance in the light and thought about Deborah Greene.

Katherine Warden had said that Turner and Greene had once been very close but had drifted apart after Turner had left the Weather Undergroud in 1973. Greene had stayed in the movement longer, drifting around the country working menial jobs under an assumed name and attending endless political meetings. I remembered a film from the mid-seventies, *Message from the Darkness*, that had featured interviews with the Weathermen. Greene had appeared with her hair cropped short, dressed in baggy work clothes, face blunt and features harsh with anger. Shortly after the film appeared, Greene broke with the Weathermen and surfaced in Montreal. While studying at McGill University she wrote a memoir denouncing the radical left for sexism and articulating her own discovery of her lesbian sexuality. She quickly became a well-known figure in feminist circles in Canada.

After half an hour or so two women walked through the lobby. One, obviously a student, was a washed-out blonde in a shapeless sweater. The other woman was striking: a figure in a suit of rich brown tweed, a face with high cheekbones and luminous dark eyes, lustrous black hair loosely curled and shot with gray. She was saying, "You're right, Marlas, it should be done. I'm having dinner with the minister tomorrow night. I'll talk to her about a grant. Good-bye."

The woman in brown turned to me and said, "You must be Mr. Riordan. How can I help you?"

I said, stupidly. "Thank you, but I'm waiting for Professor Greene."

"But I am Deborah Greene." She looked momentarily puzzled, then her voice got cold as she led me to her office. "I think you fell over a stereotype, Mr. Riordan. Just what were you expecting?"

"Someone more along the lines of the cliché, I guess. Broad shoulders. A tattoo saying 'Mom.' No visible sense of humor."

She stood rigidly behind her desk and looked at me, her face hard. "Are you one of those who just drops by to bait me?"

"No. Nor to be baited. I didn't recognize you, Ms. Greene. The last picture I saw of you was taken in 1973. Your friends had just blown up an armory. You hadn't started shopping at Bloomingdales."

She sat down and lit a thin brown cigarette and blew a thin plume of smoke at the window. "Okay." She sighed. We both made honest mistakes, and we'll forget them. What can I do for you, Mr. Riordan?"

"I want to talk to you about an old friend of yours, Stephen Turner. I'm not a cop. I'm a lawyer, working for his sister. She wants to know who killed him. She thought you might be willing to help."

Her face grew dark and somber. After a long time she said in a small quiet voice, "If I can. I hope I can."

"You knew that he'd been killed?"

"Yes. Kate called and I saw it in the papers. I didn't go to the funeral. I can't travel in the States. There are . . . some of the statutes of limitation haven't run out yet."

"What kind of person was Turner?"

"Every person you ask will give you a different answer to that question, Mr. Riordan. Most of us got a little tarnished as we got older, driven by our insecurities over money and power and sex. Steven didn't, somehow. As if he had always had his face turned to the morning."

"So you stayed close friends?"

Her eyes were dark, shining with tears. She said softly, "I loved him. In the ways that I could. And he loved me."

Deborah Greene said she could use a drink, and I had many more questions, so we drove to the east side of Victoria and wound along the shore into the suburb of Oak Bay. Victoria is more British than half of London and Oak Bay looked like Hampstead or Golders Green, a retirement posting for old soldiers of the Empire. We drove in silence down narrow streets under leafy elms and larches, past stodgy half-timbered houses with rolling green lawns, until we reached the Oak Bay Beach Hotel. We settled in at a corner table in the low-ceilinged pub, close to the fire to burn away the damp, ordered Scotch, and started in again.

"How much do you know about the killing?" I asked.

"Just what the local papers have said. SEATTLE MAN DIES IN TERRORIST SHOOT-OUT, that kind of thing. Katherine couldn't tell me much more than that when I talked to her."

"When did you last see Turner?"

"About five months ago. That was a long time for us. He usually came up to see me every two or three months on average. And we talked on the phone."

"How did he seem to you then?"

"Good. He had just broken off a relationship, one that hurt him. But he liked his work, felt it was useful. He was even getting politically active again, the nuclear freeze movement. He felt enough time had passed that his background wouldn't be an issue."

"And later, on the telephone?"

"The same. A little more preoccupied with work, things weren't going all that well for him. He really didn't say."

"Any fears? Threats he'd received?"

"No, nothing like that."

"Tell me," I said, "about how you met and got involved in student politics."

"We met in 1968," she said slowly, "our second year at the university. Steve was rooming with George Shields and both of them came to an antiwar rally with Janice Ivie and Diane Olmstead. The next year we all moved into a big old house on Capitol Hill with Danny Schoen. The rent was cheap, and we were shedding the last vestiges of the bourgeois conventions of our middle-class existence."

I smiled and said, "I'd forgotten that people used to talk like that. What does it mean?"

"Mostly it meant that George Shields got to fuck everybody," she said evenly. She finished her drink and gestured for another. "We sat around reading Mao and Che and holding self-criticism sessions and thinking about the revolution. Very political. A lot of people coming through from the national SDS leadership crashed with us, Paul

Reid and Liz Doheny and even Hal Maltzman. We were gonna make the revolution." She smiled ruefully. "I know, I know, it sounds silly after all this time. But we were so very serious then. And yet, those were some of the best times I ever had. I remember spending nights in tears; sexually I was so confused; and Steve or Blake would just get me high and hold me in their arms all night long." She shook her head slowly, as if puzzled by the passage of time.

I was about to get caught up on my own regretting, so I tried to pull the conversation back around to the facts. "When did the demonstrations start in Seattle?"

"Oh, for us that was mostly after Chicago. The big demonstrations were in '70, after the Cambodian bombing, and then the Christmas bombing and mining of Haiphong in December '71."

"The trial was in September of '71?"

"Yes."

"Were you guilty?"

"That pompous asshole Hartlett tried to lynch us. He—"

"But he didn't," I cut in. "You had the best lawyers money can buy and they put on a meticulous, powerful defense. And you got off. You can't be prosecuted again. Were you guilty?"

"No," she said slowly. She was on her third or fourth drink but was becoming more cautious as we crossed the line from conversation to questioning. She leaned forward on the table on her elbows, staring at me intently, bracing herself for what came next.

"No, what?" I said sharply.

"No, I'm not going to drag it out again, Mr. Riordan. I don't know you; don't know if I can trust you. You can't even tell me if all this ancient history has anything to do with Steve's death. I've repudiated what I've done. It was a hard thing to admit, but I did it. And I've worked much too damned hard to get where I am. I started out ten years behind, but I've made it. And I'm not going to throw it away."

I pushed at her for a while, digging into Turner's brief disappearance into the Weather Underground and her own time spent underground. Her answers got shorter until she was stonewalling in the best tradition of Nixon himself. After a while I gave it up.

"Look," she said finally. "You're not going to get anywhere with this. The movement is dead. We turned out to be no better than anybody else. We have quiet, comfortable middle-class lives. I teach school. George Shields is a rich right-wing lawyer. Diane Olmstead plays tennis and drives a BMW. It's as if the protests, the bombings, never happened."

"Not quite. Stephen Turner is dead. And look at it this way. Somebody went to a lot of trouble and expense to kill Turner. He was killed in a particularly public and particularly nasty way; shot down on a street in front of maybe thirty witnesses. Then a terrorist group takes credit for an obviously professional job. Why? Most of his life he was an ordinary person. But for three years he did extraordinary things. Led marches and rallies. Went underground. Suspected of bombing a federal courthouse, a dam, and a powerline substation. I'm looking for the reasons why someone wanted to kill him bad enough to stage a public execution. It makes the most sense to look at those years."

"I'm not sure I agree."

"I'm not asking you to. All I'm asking is for you to tell

me if there's anything, anything at all, that you know or have heard that might give me a reason why he was killed." I reached across the table and took her hand. She stiffened but didn't pull away. "You said you loved him, once. I don't know what kind of relationship you had. From what you've said it was a good one. It seems to me you owe him something. At least that much."

Her eyes were opaque. Finally she said softly, "I did love him, you know. But . . . I am a lesbian. It's what I am, and we could never really be lovers. I . . . tried. There was nothing there."

She finished her drink and stood up. She said, "I'm going home. To think. Stay here; get a room. I'll call you in the morning."

She walked away into a night of hard autumn rain, the kind of night that makes you feel cold even if you aren't. I was. I ordered more whiskey and edged closer to the fire and stayed there alone until I thought I could sleep.

I slept badly. The whiskey brought on a fevered sweat, and I dreamt of Vietnam and other things best left forgotten. At four in the morning I was pacing the room, measuring it out—twelve by sixteen, a shitty room—and wondering whether room service was awake enough to find me a bottle of Scotch at that hour.

The phone rang twice, stopped, then rang again. When I picked it up, Deborah Greene said breathlessly, "Riordan? Oh, my God, I'm sorry; I couldn't sleep. We've got to talk, I've decided—"

"Wait," I said. "Slow down. Are you drunk, or maybe speeding?"

"I was drunk, but I'm starting to sober up. I'll be okay."

"What do you want to tell me?"

"It's about Joshua . . . it's something that could be connected with Steve's death. It was so long ago, I don't know, but it could be."

"I'll be right there. Where do you live?"

She told me. Then, her voice steady, she said, "Thanks, Riordan, but I'll be okay. Get something to eat or some exercise or something, and meet me at seven. I want to take a bath and get myself together. No, it's all right. At seven." The phone clicked dead in my ear.

Deborah Greene lived a half-dozen miles north of Oak Bay in a fine little California-style bungalow that might once have been a summer retreat. It was nestled in a copse of tall cedars above a saltwater bay. It was not long after dawn, and the sky was full of soft light when I pressed the bell and got no answer. Twice. I walked around the house. The shades were drawn, and no lights were burning, giving the house a sleepy look. The only sound was the soft rhythmic slap of the waves fifty yards away. I went back to the front door to ring the bell again.

The front door was not quite shut.

I pushed it open and stepped in quietly.

Deborah Greene had spent a tough night. The air smelled of stale smoke and whiskey. In the living room an open, not-quite-empty bottle of Scotch stood uncorked on a cocktail table. A crystal ashtray overflowing with cigarette butts sat next to it.

I moved through the kitchen in the dim half light of early morning. The counters were clean, and the cabinets were closed. Nothign seemed out of place. I moved on quietly, acutely aware of the fact that I no longer wore a .38 tucked into the small of my back.

I found her in the bedroom.

She was wearing a thick white cotton robe that was black with blood from stab wounds in her chest and belly. An ordinary kitchen knife lay on the floor beside her. A bedside lamp had been knocked over. Books on a nightstand had been knocked to the floor. At least she'd had time to fight.

I went out to the kitchen and called the police, then sat on the front steps and wept until they came.

CHAPTER 8

I spent the next six bad hours with the Canadian cops.

Americans tend to think of Canada as a giant theme park. It has hills and lakes and the occasional moose. The staff speaks English with a mildly funny accent and is very polite. The water is always safe to drink.

I've never been crazy about Canada. Their cops are very tough and never had to worry about details like a Bill of Rights. They finally got a Bill of Rights last year, but the cops still don't much give a damn; all it does is slow their backswing a little when they use their nightsticks. And any country that thinks of Budweiser as an imported beer has got serious social problems.

I told my story four separate times to three separate cops, the last time to a Victoria homicide inspector named Henry Sinclair. He was fifty-five or so, as British as milk-white tea, and too old for his job, if he was any good at it. He was fleshy, with the permanently flushed face that bespeaks a long friendship with whiskey, and the mean, frightened eyes of a bureaucrat.

"Right," he said, voice clipped, as I finished my story. "Well, Mr. Riordan, I must say I don't find it credible. You claim to be conducting a private murder inquiry. She was your witness. You come into Victoria, spend one night questioning her, and she is immediately killed, just as you are going back for more questioning. By persons unknown, of course." He smirked. "Calls for some rather sizable leaps of faith, doesn't it?"

"She wasn't killed immediately," I said. My voice sounded like it belonged to someone else. A tired, patient old man. "We were in public for hours. Someone could have followed me here, made the connection. I wasn't looking for a tail. As for the rest, you can check me out with Lieutenant Vincent Ahlberg of the Seattle Police."

"Oh, we shall," he said grandly. "But suppose in the meantime we apply ourselves once more to what Miss Greene told you."

In my old man's voice, I told them again that Deborah Greene had denied any current connection with radicals in the States or in Canada, and that she didn't know who had killed Turner.

I didn't tell them about Joshua, whoever that was. It didn't mean anything to me. But the memory had been important enough or ugly enough to keep Deborah up, tired and drunk and sad, walking the floor on a cold, dim, lonely morning. If there was a thread of meaning there, it would break in Sinclair's clumsy hands.

A sharp young cop named McAffee caught the omission. "I don't understand why she called you last night, if she didn't have anything new to say," he said. "Didn't she tell you why she wanted to see you again?"

I shrugged and tried to sidestep without actually lying. "She was exhausted and drunk and quite nearly hysterical," I said. "I think she just wanted someone to talk to. I stirred up a lot of memories she'd buried."

Sinclair listened and then shook his head, the same small smirk pasted on his lips. He fitted a Dunhill into a stubby black holder and lit it with an old military lighter. "Perhaps," he said, exhaling a dramatic cloud of smoke. "And perhaps not."

"Jesus H. Christ," I growled irritably. "Listen up, Colonel Blimp. I've let you play Scotland Yard for hours now, and I'm sick of it. Now get your fat ass out of that chair and either charge me or let me go home."

"McAffee," Sinclair said, his voice hard now, "put this garbage in a cell."

I stood up. McAffee took my arm. Sinclair sat rooted like an oak in his chair. "McAffee," he added lightly, "this is a dangerous prisoner. Manacle him."

McAffee cuffed me and took me away. He put me in a cell in the holding tank and let me keep my own clothes, both good signs. If they were going to hold me for a long time, they would have taken my clothes and put me in the felony tank. The holding tank wasn't bad. It was painted gray. My cell had a toilet, a washbasin, and a bunk. There were two other prisoners in the tank. Neither of them made a sound. It was a quiet weekend in Victoria.

I spent three hours in the cell. It could have been three minutes or three days. I sat on the bunk and leaned against one shoulder since my hands were still cuffed behind my back. After a while I slept fitfully, balanced on the edge between waking and sleeping.

I woke when McAffee and Sinclair walked into the cell. Sinclair looked unhappy. I stood up. "Good afternoon, colonel," I said sarcastically.

He ignored me. "We have spoken to your Lieutenant Ahlberg," he said, grinding out the words. "Unlikely as it seems, he confirms your story. Mr. McAffee here has persuaded our commander that we lack probably cause to hold you. You will have to swear in writing that you will return when needed."

I said nothing, waiting. The cell was very small. Sinclair took two slow steps across the cell toward me. We stood facing each other, toe to toe. He was going to hit me. It was just a matter of time.

"I should like to say one more thing," he began.

"Yes, colonel?" I replied.

He hit me in the belly with a short driving right. It was a better punch than I expected, and I doubled up, gasping. With an effort, I stood striaght up and smiled.

"Not good enough, colonel." I said. "Not nearly."

He turned on his heel and left the cell.

McAffee took off my cuffs and led me to his office. His name was Irish, but he was short and dark-skinned, with shiny black hair and a heavy beard shaved blue. A lot of Greek, maybe, or Portuguese. His office was small and very carefully organized. Books and manuals of criminology and police procedure were carefully arranged on a small bookshelf. His desk was clean and uncluttered. He was the kind of cop who makes me worry.

As I signed waiver forms, McAffee said, "Are you going to make a case out of this?"

"You mean the colonel slugging me?"

"Right." His face was blank and smooth. He allowed himself a small chilly smile.

"You don't like the colonel, do you, McAffee?"

"That's not the point. But I would like you to answer."

"Not if you keep him away from me."

"He's a couple of months from a pension."

I shrugged. "A bad cop is more trouble to you than he is to me."

"True. Here you are. We'll expect to see you again."

I took the ferry to the mainland, crossed the border, and drove down Interstate 5. The problem of who Joshua was kept tugging at the corners of my mind like a small spoiled child. No one by that name had surfaced at the Northwest Nine trial or in the newspapers. The name itself didn't mean anything. Joshua had been an Old Testament prophet, possibly the one with the trumpets. I would have to check. Maybe it had no meaning at all. After all, "Rosebud" had turned out to be a sled.

It was still late afternoon when I stopped for gas in Marysville, Washington. Marysville is not much of a town, but it stands where the coastal plain begins to break up into the rolling wooded foothills of the Cascade Range. Small, neat farms dot the river valleys. In the mornings the fog hangs low over the fields. I got out and stretched and looked up at the foothills rolling on up the range, glowing with golden aspen and alder.

I didn't have to do this. I had a backpack and hiking boots in the back of my car. I could pick up a cold six-pack and turn east on the North Cascades Highway. In two hours up the road there is a tourist town called Leavenworth in a high mountain valley. I could get a good German meal and spend the night shooting pool. In the morning I could hike a long way up a mountain canyon and rinse out my drip-dry soul in the cold diamond waters of Icicle Creek.

Goddammit.

I found a pay phone and dialed a number from memory. After a long time it was answered.

"Bernstein?" I asked.

"Yeah. That you, Matthew?"

"Sure is. I've got work out here. It pays well."

"Monday okay?"

"Now would be better. If I get dead between now and then, it's your fault."

Bernstein chuckled, and I could hear the silver sound of a woman's laughter in the background. "Relax, man," he said. "Nobody works weekends anymore. Not even the bad guys. You'll be okay." I felt tired and chewed up, more lonely than I thought I could, when his chuckle faded and the phone went dead. Nothing to do but go home.

By the time I got back to Seattle, the rain had stopped, but the streets were still slick and shining. As I turned off the highway to the west on Forty-fifth Street, I could see the Olympic Mountains gleaming through the cloud breaks with the last light of sunset. Below me, down the long hill to the Sound, the headlights of hundreds of cars flicked on and flowed together, forming a river of light.

I owed myself a night at home, a quiet drink, and a long, hot shower. But I couldn't let it go. Deborah Greene had gotten killed because I had come fumbling around asking questions without taking even minimum precautions about being followed. Now I had to do what I could, whether it was nothing or everything, to find Turner's killer. And hers.

So I rolled down the hill toward the water, and joined into that river of light.

I caught up with Kyle Parman at the third tavern I tried, a fisherman's joint called the Valhalla down on Market Street in Ballard. Ballard is old town, Swede town, fishing town. It is a quiet, unflashy place of plain old houses on plain streets, where people still just do their jobs and raise their kids and hope for a decent break. It's probably the last neighborhood in Seattle where you can light a cigarette in a bar without immediately being placed on the same social scale as, say, a child molester.

The years had been hard on Kyle Parman. He wore his graying hair long and pulled back in a ponytail. His skin was a bad color, even in the dim barroom light. There were too many lines around his eyes. His knuckles and wrists were thick and lumpy as rocks, the hands of a man who works with machinery all day long. But they still moved smoothly as Parman's cue stick flashed and the balls clicked, ending a game of nine ball with a deft two-bank shot.

Parman finished his game and walked over to the bar. I stepped in front of him and said, "Kyle Parman?"

"That's right. Who the hell are you?"

"My name's Riordan. I'd like to talk to you about Stephen Turner."

"You another cop?"

"Worse. I'm a lawyer."

He gave me a slow once-over as he shook loose a Chesterfield from a crumpled pack and lit it with a kitchen match. Blowing smoke out of the corner of his mouth, he said, "Why should I talk to you?"

"Cause you can talk to me or the cops again, and me is easier."

He shrugged. "Fair enough. Hey, Benji," he shouted to another man at the pool table, "take the table. See if you can keep it this time."

I bought a pitcher of beer and followed him over to a corner booth. As I poured a couple of glasses, I said, "You know that Turner was killed, right?"

"Saw it on TV. Cops came around afterward. Didn't have much to tell them, or you." He drained one glass of beer and poured another.

"Deborah Greene got killed last night, too."

His face clenched up like a fist. He shook his head sadly. "Oh, Goddammit," he said softly. "I am so sorry to hear that. I liked the lady. How did it happen?"

"She was stabbed. About six hours after I talked to her."

"What the hell for, man?" he asked angrily. "Because they didn't like her politics? Or the people she slept with?"

"I was hoping you could tell me."

"No way, man," he said, lifting his glass again. "I'm sorry as hell about both Steve and Deb, man, but I can't help you. I don't know what this has to do with me." He leaned back in the booth, lighting another cigarette, moving the fact of death a little further away, out where he could see it and shape it in ways that wouldn't hurt him.

"Maybe nothing. Maybe a lot," I said, answering his question. "I think the killings are connected. And that the connection has something to do with the Northwest Nine trial."

"Oh, bullshit," he said with a voice of tired irritation. "That was all over, Riordan. A hundred years ago. Still, you want to buy the beer, we can talk."

"Okay," I said, ordering another pitcher. "When did you meet Turner and the others?"

"Let's see . . . 1969. I was just out of Monroe, did a year turn for assault. Parole board offered me a deal. Said I could take their money and go to the university and get me a nice student deferment or else stay inside for another year and then get shipped off to 'Nam." He laughed sarcastically. "Such a hard choice, right? So I'm off to be Joe College. I go to the unviersity and don't know what to do, so I sign up for philosophy, on a whim. And I meet Blake Riddell and Deb Greene right in my first classes."

"When did you start getting into the antiwar movement?"

"Almost right away. Blake and Deb were already active. They took me to rallies, introduced me to the people they were working with. I signed on pretty quick. People forget what a shitty war that was, especially for guys like me. I come from Colville, over on the east side of the mountains; patriotic as hell over there. Half the guys I went to school with got themselves killed or messed up in that war."

"You guys were the leaders at the university, right?"

"In a way. It was a collective."

"Where'd you fit in?"

"I was the house greaseball," he laughed, "the kid from the wrong side of the tracks. And I was useful, having had a certain working knowledge about the pigs. Sometimes I felt a little outside, but not too much. They accepted me. Besides, how many of the fucking frats were going to pledge a convicted felon?"

"How about the others?"

"Well, Turner and Greene and Shields, that son of a bitch, they were the real leaders. The rest of us just sort of hung with them."

"What's the matter with Shields?" I asked.

"Jesus. That fucker'd sell his own mother for a little of the ol' power and glory. Which is what he's doing now, running for Congress as a right-winger. And that pimp he hung around with. Danny Schoen." He snorted with disgust.

"They still friends? Shields and Schoen, I mean?"

"Christ, how would I know? I doubt it. George'd just get rid of anybody who couldn't help him get what he wants. Danny Schoen wouldn't help his political image."

"Tell me about the Northwest Nine trial," I said.

"It was a roust, pure and simple. They never had any damned evidence at all."

"Yeah, but what about the bombings? They happened. Somebody did them."

"Oh, there was talk about it all right, all the time. We had a few folks from the Weather Underground come through, and I know the people who did the post-office bombings in Portland in '70. There were some pretty crazy folks up in the mountains in those days. You could ask Shields about that: he used to let them crash up at a farmhouse his folks owned up in Roslyn, that old coal-mining town in the Cascades. But as far as I know, it never got further then talk. At least not for me."

"Could Turner and Shields and some of the others have taken part in the bombings without you knowing about it?"

He hesitated, then said, "It's possible. I wondered about that. You know, I worked hard for the movement for a long time. Harder than I had at anything. And I'm proud of that part of my life. But I was a little too old, a little too burned out to really believe that we were going to change the world. Stopping the war was enough. But you know, Turner and Deb and Blake and Janice, they really did believe they could." He laughed, but it was a short, bitter laugh, hollow and painful.

I bought us a six-pack, and we went out back to the parking lot. We sat on the trunk of Kyle's old Firebird and split a couple of joints and let our talk drift around to other things.

"How come you didn't stay with philosophy?" I asked.

"Oh, I have," he replied. "Cars are logical systems, like all machines. Some just have more elegant logic. Some don't. Take Fords. Not elegant at all."

"I'm serious," I said, laughing.

"So am I," he said. His voice got low and bitter. "I was broke, man, but I was up for a teaching assistant job that would carry through to my master's. Then we got busted. All the others were nice upper-class kids with rich families that came to the rescue. I was a two-time loser. And they stuck me. We all got acquitted. Turner paid my lawyer. But I had no job, no chance after that. It all just up and blew away."

A little while later I said, "I've just got one more thing to ask you about. Deborah Greene called me a couple of hours before she was killed. She was very sad and very drunk. She said she'd decided to tell me about Joshua, because that could be tied to Steve Turner's murder. What was she talking about? Do you know who she meant?"

He was just a bit too casual.

"Beats me," he said, suddenly sober. "I knew a few

guys named Joshua, Josh, but I don't think they knew Turner or were heavy in the movement.''

"Where are they now?"

"Hell, how would I know? Fifteen years is forever to me, man. Sorry.''

I had used Kyle Parman up. Whatever else he knew was behind a smooth blank wall. We drank some more beer and smoked some more dope, and eventually I said to hell with it and went home.

CHAPTER 9

I woke up the next morning with a nasty marijuana headache, a queasy stomach, and lungs that felt like they were full of used scar tissue. As I rolled out of bed, I could hear various parts of my body creak like an old door. Something had to be done.

I drank a quart of orange juice and shuffled slowly into old gray sweats that still had YALE FOOTBALL stenciled faintly on the chest and thigh. As I went out the door, I hazarded a look in the front hall mirror. With my bloodshot eyes, tangled brown hair, and battered sweats I could compete for the Salvation Army Track Club. At the rate I was going, someday I would.

When I started running in 1972, it was called roadwork, and it was something you did to keep your wind and legs in shape for football or skiing or whatever. You didn't wear Day-Glo fashion-colored warm-up suits and bore people with tales of your latest 10k race while sipping

Perrier at a cocktail party. You just did it and ignored the funny looks you got from people in the neighborhood.

But I had stuck with it through the years when I drank and smoked heavily, and it seemed to keep the moving parts in working order. Maybe the trendy health types had a point after all.

It wasn't yet eight, and the morning fog was still settled into the low spots like thick ropes of cotton as I jogged slowly south on the Burke-Gilman Trail. The trail is an old railbed, now asphalt-paved, that winds east from Lake Union, past the university, and north along the west shore of Lake Washington. Even in winter it is a patch of life in the city, and in mid-September it was still a cool green tunnel through arching alders and Chinese elms along the foot of the bluff above the lake.

In the first mile I tottered along like the tin man; I would have lost a race to an eighty-year-old grandmother carrying a bag of groceries. The second mile wasn't much better. But the sun warmed my back, and the sweat began to flow, and my feet slapped out a steady rhythm along the gravel path, and I felt well.

At Matthews Beach Park, three miles down the trail, I turned off the path and sprinted up the small hill dividing the trail from the park, then stretched out my stride, careless as a child, and ran easily down the long grassy slope to the lake.

At the beach I stopped and splashed my face with cold water, looking out at the lake. The last of the fog clung to the smooth surface of the lake, but the Cascade Mountains stood out clearly, positively gaudy in their first coat of autumn snow.

I heard the swimmer before I saw her. She was at the far

end of the beach, swimming a strong, smooth crawl in the cold September water between two strings of buoys a hundred yards apart. She swam another couple of laps and them swam toward shore, standing up in the shallows and walking toward the beach. She wore an old black one-piece Speedo racing suit, a garment that tried to make women sexless but failed magnificently. She had slender but strong shoulders. Her breasts were full but flattened by the suit. Her hips switched gently as she walked slowly through the water. As she pulled off a swimcap, a mass of blond hair tumbled down, and suddenly I recognized Katherine Warden.

I stood by her bicycle and waited as she walked up.

"Hello," I said.

She gave me a warm but puzzled smile and said, "Hello, Matthew. What are you doing here?"

"Waiting for you," I said, smiling.

She gave that another smile and wrapped herself in a heavy towel. She took a sweatsuit out of a bicycle basket. "Wait for me while I change," she said. "I'd like to talk."

When she came back from the beach shelter, I said, "I live just a couple miles north of here, on the beach. Would you like some coffee? Or some breakfast? You could ride your bike there."

"Can you run alongside?"

"I'm old," I said, shuffling into a jog, "but not decrepit."

When we were back on the trail, I asked, "What's with the swimming? Lake Washington doesn't get much above sixty degrees, even in the summer."

"My father used to swim in the lake every day, even in the winter," she answered. "He started me and Steve

71

when we were kids. I swam in high school and college, too. I just never stopped. You really don't notice the cold. Try it sometime.''

''Thanks,'' I said, grinning, ''but I've got other ways of doing penance for my sins.''

She smiled a reply and concentrated on her riding. In the days since I had last seen her, time had washed a lot of the gaunt, grim look of pain out of her face. Her skin was tan, her brown eyes clear in the morning light. She looked back at me and caught me watching her, but her smile was still as generous as before.

I was living that year in a small wooden house that sheltered in a madrona thicket on the northwest shore of Lake Washington. The house had been built before World War II by my aunt, an iron-willed maiden lady artist and teacher. She found the local builders too dear and too patronizing, so she ordered a manual on wood-home construction from the U.S. Government's Forest Product Laboratory in Madison, Wisconsin, a pile of timber, and some Sears & Roebuck tools. The house was squarish and plain, like she was. But it was set on deeply driven piles and strongly built; whenever she was in doubt, she would just double the dimension and double the lumber.

My aunt died and willed me the house the summer before I left New York. The house and her students were her only memorial. There are worse ones. Perhaps once a year, usually on a November day of bitter rain, one of her students, grown middle-aged and balding, shows up at my door and shyly asks if Miss McKenna still lives there. I make them tea and whiskey, and they tell me stories about the woman who taught them the pleasure of looking at the world with an open mind, so they could see the beauty there.

By the time I got out of the shower the driftwood fire was going, and the coffee was done. I poured two white mugs and gave one to Kate as she stood by the fire. She took it, smiling, and kissed me quickly on the corner of the mouth, then sat on the sofa, curling her legs beneath her. I sat down beside her.

"This is a very nice house," she said. "It's full of light."

"The woman who built it was an artist, a painter. She needed the south light. She said it took her from 1939 to 1946 to get those skylights to stop leaking."

"She must have been practical, for an artist."

"She was, I guess. She thought a painting had to be built up with strong joints, no matter what kind of painting it was. She built this house the same way."

Kate drank some coffee and said, "For all the checking I've done into your background, I still don't know you very well. I'd like to. Would you tell me more about yourself? Or is that asking too much?"

"It isn't asking anything," I replied. "It's just not something I'm good at doing. I can't tell you any great and guiding principles I live my life by, because I'm not sure I believe in any anymore. All I can do is tell you what I like or don't like."

"What do you like?" she asked.

"Beer. Sunday afternoon naps after reading *The New York Times*. Women. Not necessarily in that order."

"That's good to know," she said, grinning. "Do you have a woman in your life now?" When I didn't answer her right away, she said, "And that's none of my business, right?"

"There isn't one, not now, anyway," I answered. "I'm not very eligible, I'm afraid. In a way it's funny. When I was twenty-years-old and in the army, all I wanted was a house and a wife and kids and to be a junior partner in some big law firm. But the times weren't right for that, and nothing worked out then. Now everybody wants the suburbs and kids again. But I think I'm too old and too mean for all that."

"Times change," she replied. "There are different kinds of marriages now, or at least different ways of working at them. It can be a state of grace." She smiled ruefully. "I sound like Dear Abby. But don't fall in love with your own splendid solitude, Matthew. It's harder than you think."

She didn't say anything else, and the silence hung awkwardly between us. We were both acutely aware that we were alone in my house and that neither of us much gave a damn if virtue triumphed.

I finally broke the silence. "I should bring you up-to-date on what I've been doing on the investigation. I wasn't in very good shape when I called you last night. I liked Deborah Greene. Very much. Her death hit me pretty hard."

Kate's smile fell away. She jerked herself rigidly to her feet. "Stop!" she hissed. "Please, please, stop. Why are you doing this to me? I have had half a life full of living with death. My parents, my husband, my daughter, my brother. For a few bright hours this morning I hadn't thought about them. I was happy just being with you. Couldn't you see that? And now all you can do is tell me more about death. You bastard."

She walked away, stiffly. She stood rigidly in front of a window, staring blindly through it. Her hands were clenched into fists so hard that they shook.

I walked up behind her and put my arms around her.

"Don't you know," I said, my own voice breaking, "that I would give anything to have met you at some other time, in some other place? So that I wouldn't know that I was always going to remind you, just by being there, of the ugly way your brother died?"

She didn't say anything. She simply turned around and came into my arms. She kissed me slowly, as if we had all the time in the world together. And then again. Her eyes were shining.

But with tears.

An hour later she stretched out a bare arm and stroked my cheek. She had a smile that combined affection and humor and maybe even a little love. It was a smile that could sell a million cars or a million bottles of gin, and I basked in its warmth.

"What are you thinking?" she asked.

"That I know how that guy Botticelli felt."

"Botticelli, the painter?"

"Uh-huh. The one who painted the blonde coming out of the water."

She slapped me on the belly. Not too gently.

"Conceit," she said with mock anger. "Reeking *male* conceit. If you could talk to a five-hundred-year-old Italian painter, you'd be just a couple of the guys, sitting around swapping stories about getting laid. Jesus." She put a hand over my mouth to stifle my laughter. "No depth, Riordan, none at all."

"The sensitive New Man is out. Women are back into tough guys again," I said.

"Are you a tough guy, Riordan?"

"Of course."

"How are you going to prove it?"

"Won't. If you have to prove it, you're not tough. Tough guys are existential, too."

We laughed together. Katherine propped herself up on her elbows and looked down at me. Her eyes were wide and searching.

I reached up and pulled her down close to me before she could ask the questions we both wanted to ask. When I had her settled under one arm, I stroked her forehead with my free hand, smoothing her hair back from the brow.

She closed her eyes. "My mother used to do that," she whispered, "whenever I was lonely or afraid. It still feels nice."

"Good."

"So, what do we do now, Matthew?"

"I know what I want to do. It may not be the right thing to do."

"What's that?"

"Leave with me. Now. Today. We can be down in Mexico, Cabo San Lucas or someplace else warm, by tonight. It doesn't matter right now who loves who or how much. We can settle all that later. But we have to go, now."

She thought about that for a very long time. Finally, she said, in a small, pained voice, "I can't. You saw what they did to Steve. I've got to see this thing through. That's the right thing to do, isn't it?"

"I don't know. I think so."

"I need your help to do this."

"I know. I'll be here."

After a while we got up and had more coffee and breakfast together. We were cheerful, and Katherine's bright laughter filled my house. Eventually I took her home.

Knowing that sometimes one chance is all you get.

CHAPTER 10

Fifteen years ago, when I first saw it, the battered old tavern on an empty stretch of Pacific Highway South between Seattle and Tacoma had been the South Side Inn. It was a reasonably friendly workingman's joint that poured draft Rainier beer, cheap red wine, and, if the bartender liked your looks enough to forget the liquor laws, quick shots of Old Granddad from under the bar. It was nothing to look at, but the pool tables were level, the cues straight, and the crowd quiet.

Fifteen years is hard on people but harder on cities. The Pacific Highway is now an artery through the vile mess of pizza shops and used-car lots that sprawls south of the city. The South Side was long gone, existing only in the memory of scared young soldier boys like me who were shipping out from Fort Lewis to Vietnam. Now it was called Danny's Place. A cheap new stucco front had been pasted on the sagging building, like makeup on an aging actor. A four-foot sign spelled TOPLESS in red neon letters that could be seen a mile away even through the electric sleaze bordering the highway.

Inside, the air was thick with smoke. Metallic rock music pounded. Red strobe lights glared on a mirrored stage. Even the walls were red, covered with enough fake red plush to put a crooked fire inspector's kids through Johns Hopkins.

The early Saturday-night crowd of polyester suburbanites and bored soldiers watched a dancer on the stage. She was a slender black woman with pendulous breasts. She barely swayed to the music. She peeled off her T-shirt and dropped it on the floor to lonely scattered applause from a half-dozen tables. The dancer ignored the applause and stared straight ahead, as if stoned on something unique and awful.

A half-dozen other women danced at tables lined up along the walls. I took a chair at one of these and sat down. A short, stocky little brunette wearing bikini panties and a see-through pajama top detached herself from a cluster of women at the bar and wobbled on too-high heels over to my table.

"Want a drink?" she shouted over the music.

"Beer," I yelled back.

"No booze," she answered. "The Liquor Board says we're too lewd," she added, giggling.

She went and got a couple of shotglass-sized three-dollar Cokes instead. She sat down next to me and asked about my name and business while indulging in more random body contact than is usually found in public places.

"Want me to dance for you?" she asked.

"No, thanks. I want—"

"Are you *sure*?" she said, breathily, her eyes holding mine. She slid from behind the table and stood in front of me. She slowly untied her top and lifted one of her heavy breasts to her mouth. She flicked at the nipple with a fat pink tongue. She was all of maybe nineteen.

"I'm sure," I said.

Her expression abruptly changed to flat boredom. "Free show's over, Jack," she said as she started to turn away.

I waved a twenty-dollar bill at her, lazily. She quickly sat back down.

"What's your pleasure?" she asked.

"Danny around?"

"Don't know. I got on at four and haven't seen him. He'd be back in his office, probably."

"Doing what?"

"Interviewing new talent," she said scornfully. "And trying to stuff his dick down her throat."

"Where's the office?"

"Behind the bar. There's a door back by the men's can."

"Has Danny got a floor manager?"

"The big guy with the beard," she replied, starting to glance around.

"Tell me about him."

"Hey, look. I don't know what this is about, but I don't need any trouble."

I was still holding the twenty. I started folding it up with one hand. She put a hand over mine.

"Don't hurry away, man. His name's Eddie Bogan. He's been with Danny about a year. He's a lousy fuck. I don't know much more than that."

"Tell him I want to see him."

I opened my hand and she took the bill, folding it small, and slipping it in her panties before she wobbled away.

Eddie drifted over about ten minutes later. He was big, six-feet, and maybe 220, but a lot of it was great rolling gut that spilled over his belt. He pulled out a chair, reversed it, and straddled it. He eyed me carefully. I didn't fit in with his usual customers, the eighteen-year-old dog soldiers or the bleary-eyed businessmen. I was dressed in my best lounge-lizard clothes. Short leather jacket. Designer jeans. Snakeskin boots. And a small, flat, nearly inconspicuous .32 automatic.

"So what's the score, man?" he said at last. "The ladies not up to your standards?"

"I appreciate all the little mamas, man," I drawled, "but what I want is to talk to Danny."

"Danny's busy. Talk to me."

"No." I shrugged. "It's your ass."

"Come on, man, give me some idea of what you're about. We're exposed here."

That made sense. "You must be Ed, right?"

"That's right. So?"

"I hear good things about you, Eddie. Anyway, I'm down from Alaska. We want you and Danny to supply us some ladies."

"Dancers?"

"And other things, my man." I threw in a nasty chuckle. "You show the little mamas the door at sixty below, they tend to do what they're told."

Eddie laughed. Small and mean. "Oh, I do like your style," he said. He dropped his voice. "You're with Nick, right?"

I gave him a hard look. "Big Nick's on an extended

vacation. At Lompoc. All expenses federally paid. Fresh air, exercise, time enough to get those little things done." I put my hands flat on the table. "So, no more shit, okay, Eddie? I'm the new outfit. What do you want, a business card? A company ID? Now get me Danny."

He made a placating gesture, hands up, palms out. "Sorry, man," he said. "But I had to check you out. Danny's uh, interviewing some new talent." He checked his watch, leering. "But he ought to be done by now. Come on."

Eddie led me back to the office behind the car. He knocked softly and we walked in.

Danny Schoen was sitting in a high-backed vinyl office chair behind a cheap plastic fake wood desk. His head was thrown back against the chair, and his eyes were closed.

A thin blond woman knelt in front of him. Her head bobbed up and down between his thighs.

He grunted. The grunt turned into a moan and slipped away as a sigh. The blonde stood up and wiped her face. She turned and looked at us as she slipped into a pair of jeans. She didn't say anything. After a while all humiliations are the same.

Danny Schoen said, "That was all right, Tracy. You start Monday. Noon shift. Pretty good tips."

The woman said okay, and left.

Schoen opened his eyes and saw us. He turned his chair away to button his pants, shouting, "What the fuck goes here, Eddie? I told you I was checking talent. What do I have to do, put up a sign? Who the fuck is this?"

"He's the guy taking over for Nick in Anchorage, Dan. Wants to talk some business."

"Yeah? Well, okay." Schoen stepped around his desk

and shook my hand. He was only five seven or so, and thin. He had a long, narrow face. His dirty-blond hair was swept back in a near ducktail, just like his old newspaper photos. He looked like an aging, lecherous teenager. Not tough, perhaps. But surely mean.

He motioned me to a chair. I sat. So did Eddie. I looked at him steadily. Schoen said, "Eddie, go check out Tracy, the one that was here. Get her a costume and make sure she knows the drill, okay?"

Eddie lumbered out.

"Let's get to it," Schoen said.

"Sure. I'm not from Alaska, and I don't want any girls. I'm not a cop. My name's Riordan, and I'm here to ask you questions about why Steve Turner got blown away two weeks ago."

Schoen leaned back in his chair and said calmly, "Get out now, Riordan. Right now. While you can still walk."

"Wrong play, Dan," I said conversationally. "Tough, but not smart. I've got pull on this thing. Throw me out now and you'll be picked up anytime you go into King County. The Seattle cops will ask you questions for about eight straight days, and they'll do it in places where your lawyers won't be able to find you. I have the feeling that Seattle will be happy to see you again."

"Or what?" He sighed. "We just talk?"

"Good thinking, Danny. Every problem an opportunity. We talk. Off the record. About Turner."

"Not much to talk about," he said. He took a long cigarette from a box on his desk and lit it, wreathing himself in smoke. He looked bored.

"When was the last time you saw Turner?"

"Couple years ago, maybe. Just after I got out of

MacNeill Island.'' He laughed sarcastically. "It's sad. Two old friends, and our lives just don't come together anymore.''

"How about the others who were in the Nine? Do you see them?"

"Not much. I wouldn't mind seeing Diane, though. A sweet piece of ass, Diane.''

"What about George Shields?''

"Yeah, I see George around. Occasionally.''

"You a born-again Christian, too?''

He laughed again, merrily. It was a game, and Danny was starting to enjoy it. I was not.

"That's just a shuck,'' he said. "Old George and me, we're much alike. We both learned from Chairman Mao, way back in our young radical days, that power is the only thing worth having. Doesn't matter much how you get it.''

"Have you got any connection with this new group, the Liberation Faction? They took credit for the shooting.''

"I'm a capitalist, man. I do money, not politics. I can put the word out on the street for you, see what I can pick up. But I don't know anything about them.''

"What you're telling me, if I've got it right, is that you haven't seen Turner for years, have no connections with him, and don't know who killed him, or why. Correct?"

"Oh, very good, pal. Most astute.''

"Then, tell me why he had half a pound of your cocaine in his apartment when he died.''

His face got very hard. "What kind of bullshit is this?'' he exploded, then said, more calmly, "I don't know anything about cocaine, Riordan.''

I shook my head. "I'm too old to listen to horseshit, Danny. You're running so much snow out of here, you're going to have to put in a chair lift and a bunny hill. You're not doing it smart, and you're gonna take a fall for it soon. I don't know if you killed Turner. I doubt it. But somebody is making it look like Turner was dealing for you. And that makes you the perfect candidate to get tagged for the job. You're just too dumb to see that."

His face had no expression, like a death mask. He picked up the telephone on his desk and spoke quietly.

"Eddie, get your ass in here and throw this motherfucker out," he said. "Now. So hard he bounces."

I stayed in my chair. I briefly thought about playing it easy and trying to walk out. I would not make it to the door. For reasons of his own, Danny Schoen wanted me hurt.

Eddie came in, running. "What's the problem, Danny?"

"He's not from Alaska, you clown. He's a lawyer, for crissakes. You let him in. Now throw him out."

Eddie scowled at me. "Out of the chair, scumbag."

I smiled.

He grabbed me by the collar and tried to jerk me out of the chair. It didn't work. I'm not small, six-foot-three and a hundred-ninety pounds. He was going to have to use a lot of leverage to haul me out of the chair. When he shifted his weight back to bring me up, I went with the pull.

I hit him twice in his soft belly as he stumbled backward. He doubled over, gasping. I grabbed him by the back of the neck and pulled him down and put a knee in his face. He grunted with pain, but he came up and burrowed in like a hurt fighter in the clinch, going for my kidneys. I brought both arms back inside and pushed on his face and broke his hold.

He stumbled back against the wall and tried to reach inside his jacket. I pinned his arms back and used my knees. He started to sag. I reached into his jacket and ripped a short-barreled .38 out of his holster. Eddie slid down on the floor, huffing like a steam engine and gently holding his crotch. I thumbed the safety off Eddie's .38 and showed it to him. He was very still and attentive.

"No trouble," he said, shaking his head.

I stood up and pointed the gun at Schoen and waited for the breath to stop rattling around in my chest.

Schoen was sitting at his desk, stone-faced. As I backed toward the door, I said, "Think about it, Dan. The cops are going to connect you and Turner sooner or later. You're the friendly neighborhood dealer and all-round small-time hood. They'll tailor it for you."

He was unimpressed. He said, "This buys you nothing, Riordan. You're hurt. Maybe dead."

I went out the door hearing that.

CHAPTER 11

Diane Olmstead lived on a houseboat that was much more house than boat—two-and-a-half stories of brown-stained cedar and bronzed glass that towered over the older, more modest boats. A gaily colored Japanese box kite dangled in the breeze from an upper-story deck. A new BMW gleamed blackly on the dock beside it. The houseboat was moored so that it looked east over the serenity of Portage Bay to the Cascade Mountains that stood bright with morning sun. It was Sunday morning and I could almost hear the rustle of *The New York Times* being opened, see the kiwi fruit being sliced, smell the French roast being brewed. Yuppie heaven.

The Diane Olmstead who opened the door bore no resemblance to the sullen-mouthed jailbait blonde in the leather minidress of a dozen years before. That woman was frozen in time in Turner's old photographs. This new woman was my own age. She was tall and moved with easy grace. She wore a burgundy running suit and match-ing shoes. Her lightly curled brown hair was restrained by a runner's headband. Even though she had just finished running she wore light touches of makeup with such per-fection that she could have appeared in a white wine commercial.

"Come on in, Mr. Riordan," she said, breathing heav-ily. "I'm just finishing my cool-down exercises. Be with you in a minute, so come on back."

I followed her through a neo–Art Deco living room of dusty rose and forest green to an open deck beyond. A younger man of maybe twenty-eight stood there. He was six-feet-tall or so and whippet-thin. His face and bare upper body were still tan late in the fall, his teeth white. His hair was black and razor-styled. He was stretching his arms and shoulders, pushing at the air with a movement, I thought, from aikido.

He finished the exercise and put on a loose cotton sweater, tucking a towel carefully around his neck. Then he looked at me for the first time, smiling coldly, as arrogant as a teenage tomcat.

Jay Gatsby would have loved this guy. I had the feeling I wouldn't.

"Christoper Gordon," he announced, sitting down.

"Matthew Riordan." I didn't offer to shake hands.

He nodded at Diane as she finished stretching. "Fantas-tic lady. When we got together a year ago, she was working way too hard, too stressed out, even still smok-ing. Today she ran four miles in less than thirty minutes."

"Terrific," I agreed. "You her coach?"

"No, I'm her . . . There isn't a good word for it, is there, Riordan? We live together." He poured himself a cut-crystal glass of orange juice. "Are you a runner, Riordan?"

"As penance. Not for recreation."

"Chris is a fantastic runner," Diane Olmstead said as she pulled a robe around herself and sat down. "He's a lawyer, too. What did you want to talk about, Mr. Riordan? Something about poor Stephen, I thought you said."

"That's right. I represent Katherine Warden, Turner's sister. You already know that he was shot and killed. She's asked me to investigate his murder."

"That's rather melodramatic, isn't it?" Gordon cut in sarcastically.

"Love and death usually are," I said evenly. I turned back to Diane. "One of the things I'm doing is talking to all the defendants in the Northwest Nine trial."

Diane Olmstead sighed and said, "I was afraid that was going to be it."

Gordon cut in again. "Before you get started, Riordan, we need some ground rules here, and a game plan."

"Ground rules?" I looked at him steadily. "Game plan?"

"Yes, ground rules," he said, his voice rising. "Diane must consider all aspects of this situation. Her business and professional reputation might suffer from dredging up all this old nonsense. She has her family's feelings to consider as well. Moreover—"

"Do you," I said to Diane Olmstead, "just leave him on in the background, sort of like FM radio?"

I think she started to smile.

Gordon stood up angrily. "I don't have to take this from you," he said angrily, his face flushed.

"Then don't. Leave."

He took a step toward me. I put up a hand. I said, "I can't run a marathon with you, Chris. But I sure as shit can put you in the hospital, and I will."

He stayed where he was. Diane Olmstead said, "Darling, you need to work on your remarks for the Chamber of Commerce brunch. This isn't going to take long." Gordon waited a long minute, then turned and left.

When he was gone, I said to Diane Olmstead, "The first thing I want to do is apologize."

She shrugged. "Not necessary," she replied. "Chris can be overbearing. But he's right. I don't need bad publicity now."

"Whatever you tell me I'll keep as confidential as I can, under the law. What kind of business are you in?"

"Real estate," she replied. I should have guessed. "I'm expanding my agency from residential into commercial property. Reputation means a lot."

"I understand. When did you meet Steve Turner?"

"In '68 or '69, at the university. I was going out with George Shields then. George and I had gone together since prep school."

"Were you close to Turner then? Friends?"

"Not really," she answered. "Steve was pretty arrogant in those days. The philosopher type, you know, so very smart. You couldn't argue with him. If you didn't agree with him on something, he would just sit back and sort of smile and then destroy you. I always felt stupid around him. I think that's the way he wanted people to feel."

"Had you seen him recently, within the last year or so?"

"Not really. Once in a while around town. Nothing planned."

"How about George Shields?"

"I still like George. No romance, of course, but I still see him for lunch or a drink occasionally. I don't know whether I'll support him for Congress. He's been a friend for a long time, since we were kids. And there probably is some cachet to having slept with a Congressman." She smiled at her own joke. "But he's gone awfully right-wing lately. He's even passing himself off as a born-again Christian, for God's sake. I know times change. But not that much. Not for George."

I wanted to ask more about George Shields but was afraid that she would call and warn him if I showed any unusual interest. So I kept asking her about old names and places until I said casually, "And what about Joshua? Do you still see him?"

She tensed up. It was subtle, but it was there. She said, "I didn't know anyone named Joshua in those days. Are you sure you have the name right?"

"I think so. I got it from Kyle Parman," I lied.

"Oh, Kyle didn't always know what was really going on," she said quickly. "Anyway, the name doesn't mean much."

I thought that was a strange answer, but I let it pass.

"Ms. Olmstead," I said, "a new radical group, the Liberation Faction, took credit for shooting Turner. Do you have any connection with that group or other political groups today?"

She laughed merrily. "Oh, come on, Mr. Riordan, take a look around you!" She waved a hand at her living room with its gleaming hardwood floors and Italian-leather furniture. "Does this look like an SDS crash pad to you?"

"How about the old groups?" I persisted. "Maybe sit

around with a nice white burgundy, some decent dope, and chant 'Ho, Ho, Ho Chi Minh'? Just like the old days?''

"For God's sake, Riordan," she replied. "We used to say that stuff back in 1969. You know. Where were you in '69?''

"At a fire base in Quang Tri province, South Vietnam."

"Well, shit, a Vietnam vet," she drawled acidly. "You know, you baby-killers are getting popular again. Got parades, even got your own monument. You're big-time at last."

I sat there with my jaw clamped and regretted that I was too old-fashioned to hit a woman. Before I could think of a reply, Diane Olmstead had stood up and was saying "I think you should leave, Riordan. And if one word of this leaks to the press, Chris will—"

I broke out in open laughter. "Lady, don't try to threaten me with your boy toy. It won't work. But you can relax. I'm not going to talk to you again. I know you're lying to me. You're in the real estate business, you should be better at it."

"That's got nothing—"

"Every time I mention the name Joshua to one of you, you all freeze up. Who is he? What's he got on all of you?''

"I don't know what you're talking about," she said stiffly.

"Doesn't matter. There's a Seattle homicide lieutenant who's asking the same questions. He's usually polite, but he's getting frustrated. He may decide that you need to chat with him at the cop shop. And if you try to use Boy Chris on him, that cop will make damn sure that the papers and all five TV channels are there to cover your little chat.

Maybe you can use the film they'll take of you trying to hide your face as a TV commercial.''

She led me to the door in a cold, silent fury. When I was standing on the dock, I turned back and said, "There's one other thing you should consider. Deborah Greene was going to tell me something about Joshua. Somebody killed her before she could. Until the truth comes out, you are all going to be at risk. The list could get very long, Ms. Olmstead. And you would be on it."

It was bright early morning when I left, but I felt tired and foolish. One seldom makes friends or good witnesses by insulting and threatening them. On Sunday. Before breakfast.

CHAPTER 12

At nine o'clock on Monday morning I was back in my office fiddling glumly with a pile of papers on my desk that seemed to have reproduced itself four or five times during the week I had spent playing detective. I had plowed through just enough of it to wonder for the hundredth time why we lawyers use fifty words when five will do, when Bernstein walked through my door like the hope of deliverance itself.

"Matthew," he growled cheerfully. I looked him over. Bernstein is tall and wide and dark. His beard is thick and just now going gray. His eyes are nearly black, impenetrable eyes that see much but give little. This morning they were a little bloodshot. He looked a lot like God would after a tough night in the bars.

"You had breakfast?" I asked.

"On an airplane?" He snorted in disgust. "I want some scrambled eggs. And beer. Not necessarily in that order."

"The bars around here have been open for hours" I replied with a smile. "By now the customers might even be risking a little food. Let's go."

We walked down King to First and up First to Larry's Greenfront Café. Larry's is the sort of joint, getting rarer now, where the bartender comes to work before the cook and the customers are mostly sailors who talk in ten or fifteen different languages. They make good breakfasts at any time of day and give you *salsa* for your eggs without asking. I will be sad when it is pushed out of the square. Surely the world has enough Northern Italian restaurants.

Bernstein and I ate and talked and caught up as old friends do who don't live in the same town.

I had met Bernstein in Saigon in 1970. We had gotten to know each other during a mortar attack, hiding behind the same concrete wall in the patio of the third-rate French hotel where he lived. I was waiting to get Vietnamized the hell out of there, and he was in Army intelligence, posing as a French-Jewish colonial dealing dollars and medical suppies on the black market. After the war he went to work for the CIA in Lebanon and Marseilles and other dusty, formerly French parts of the world. I saw him off and on in New York and Washington during the seventies, my friend the spook, until the night he abruptly announced his retirement by throwing his control officer a clean fifteen feet across the Oak Room Bar of the Plaza Hotel in New York. His control, a Yalie named Oakes, was still rising when he hit the wall.

After that he disappeared for two years. He does not offer, and I don't ask. In 1981 he reappeared, thinner, older, but not visibly wiser, as the best, and only, licensed private dick in Kalispell, Montana. Now he lives on a small ranch on the east side of Flathead Lake, skis a hundred days a winter, and lives far enough beyond his means that he needs to take dirty jobs like mine once in a while.

When breakfast was over, he ordered a third round of beer and leaned back, tamping a Camel on a thumbnail. He lit it and offered me the pack. I shook my head regretfully.

"You've gone righteous like everybody else," he said accusingly.

"It's not the eighties. It's the thirties."

He shrugged. "Ignore 'em and they'll go away. Suppose you tell me what this is all about."

I did, starting with the shooting in Pioneer Square and continuing into my nostalgic tour thrugh the 1960s with the members of the Northwest Nine.

When I was through, Bernstein asked, "How did these people do after the war was over?"

"As well as any other bunch of mostly upper-class white kids would do," I answered. "They grew up to be doctors and lawyers and Indian chiefs."

"And do they think about the casualties along the way?"

"Not much."

"Fuck 'em," he said. If you're right about this Joshua guy being missing all these years and possibly a witness to something, somebody may kill them all. Good. Let's go trout fishing."

"I can't walk away from it. Kate needs to know."

"You've got something for this lady?"

"Yes."

"All right," he sighed. "You've done all the record checks, reviewed the police investigation, interviewed a bunch of people, and you've got nothing so far but a sign or two that something is going on under the surface that could connect your two murders. So, what's for me to do?"

"Two things, I guess. First, keep Henry Cruz from having me killed if the itch strikes him. Second, put some pressure on when we need it. You're good at that. It's one of your best things."

Bernstein's smile was very cold. "Yes, it is. For how much?"

"Two-fifty a day, expenses. For as long as it takes. You got any pressing business back in Kalispell? Or domestic arrangements?"

"For two-fifty a day, Matthew, home is where I hang my hangover. What's the program?"

"Stake out Danny Schoen's bar. He's vulnerable because he's dirty. Try to find something we can use as a crowbar on him. After a day or two they'll make you, but that's okay. When they do, bust them up a little. Let Danny know we're thinking about him."

"No problem," he said.

As we walked back to my office, the sun broke through the morning clouds, and the rain-wet streets gleamed as if they were brand-new. I tried to enjoy the morning. I couldn't. I felt like I'd felt years ago, in the army, just before a mission: queasy and irritable, as if every nerve I had was at attention. Bringing Bernstein into the case was a sort of escalation. He would tear away at the case until he found what he was looking for, no matter what it cost. There would be no turning back.

* * *

Mustafa Kemal said on the telephone that I could see him at lunchtime while he was working out, so after Bernstein left I got my car from the garage and drove up Yesler Way through the Central District and down into the Rainier Valley. The Central District and the Valley are Seattle's ghettos, home mostly for blacks, the first ones off the boat, and the Vietnamese, the last ones off the boat. There's symmetry in that, but it's not one I understand.

I found the gym just off Rainier Avenue near King Way. It was located in an abandoned grocery store. It was not trendy. Instead of chrome-plated Nautilus machines and plush carpets it had steel bars and iron disks resting in big racks. The walls were covered with smudged mirrors and posters of black bodybuilding champions. A boxing ring was in use in one corner. I liked it. It smelled like sweat and cigar smoke, and any ad executive trying to sign up for aerobics would have been beaten up and tossed into the street.

I wasn't sure what Kemal looked like after ten years, so I looked for the manager. I found him behind a counter, sorting towels. He was black, only about six feet tall but definitely a bodybuilder. His enormous arms and chest tapered into an absurdly small waist. He looked at me with casual hostility. In this part of town white guys in three-piece suits were from the city or the county and a hassle, small or big, but always a hassle.

"Yeah," he said impatiently.

"I'm looking for Mustafa Kamal. Do you know him?"

"Does he want to see you?"

"I don't know. He said he would."

"Okay," he said slowly, thinking it over. He took me over to a freestanding rack for doing leg squats. A well-muscled man held a two-hundred-pound bar on his shoulders and squatted up and down, grunting with exertion. "Hey, 'Stafa," the manager said, "there's a honkie in a three-piece suit here to talk to you."

The man in the rack lifted the bar and set it back on the rack. "Relax, Reginald," he said without turning. "I get most of the center's money from honkies in three-piece suits."

He took a towel, stepped away from the rack and said, "I'm Mustafa Kemal. You must be Riordan."

"Right."

We shook hands and looked each other over. Kemal had been a tense, serious kid, a mixed-up Baptist divinity student who had found what he had been searcing for in radical black politics. The last picture I had seen of him showed a skinny kid with thick glasses got up in Black Panther leathers that were too big for him, face angry and fist clenched in the black-power salute. This man was relaxed, friendly, and built like a fast middleweight. Unlike the others, Kemal was not just changed. He was remade.

"Mind if I keep working out while we talk? I find lifting a good therapy for all those frustrations that build up."

"Fine. Can I help?"

"I want to do some on the bench. Do you know how to spot me?"

"Sure." I replied. We walked over to the weight benches. Kemal spread his towel on the bench below a hundred-and-ninety-pound bar. "I usually do twelve with this, but today I'm going for fifteen," he said.

"Jesus. With a hundred-ninety pounds?"

"You lift, Riordan?"

"Yeah, but not like that."

"Well, let's give it a try." Kemal lay down and grasped the bar. He drew in his breath and blew the weight up, pumping it up and down rhythmically.

He started to lose it on the fourteenth rep. I lifted a little on the bar and together we pushed it back onto the rack.

"You've almost got fifteen," I said.

"Maybe next week. I'm trying to get back to the same shape I was in at Monroe. But that was twelve years ago. And I had time to work out every day. Prison's good for that."

"What were you in for?" I asked.

"Incitement to riot and conspiracy. I was a leader in those demonstrations in the Yesler Projects in '72. Anyway, why'd you want to see me?"

"Like I said over the phone, I'm trying to find out who killed Stephen Turner. I'm talking to everybody involved in the Northwest Nine trial. What did you think of Turner, anyway?"

"Not much. A rich kid looking to assuage his guilt."

"He supported your community center. Substantially."

"So what? If you've got a lot of money, a little thrown around to the poor is nothing. That doesn't change what Turner was or what I think. But I should speak well of the dead. So here goes: He was better than the rest of them."

"In what ways?" I asked.

"I don't know. Sincerity, I guess. He was almost religious about wanting to help people. He just didn't know how to do it. He'd have made a good monk, I think."

"What about the others?"

"I don't have any use for them. Danny Schoen was—is—a pimp. George Shields is a power-hungry fascist. For the rest of them it was just an adolescent game. Look at them now. They just walked away untouched when the game was over."

"And you didn't," I said flatly.

He smiled mirthlessly. "No. I surely did not."

"Why did you get involved with the whites, then?"

"It actually worked the other way around. They sought us blacks out, wanted to tap into our revolutionary spirit. We wanted their money, their numbers, their ability to get media. Besides, when you're nineteen-years-old and trying to make a revolution, you take whatever help you can get. You don't know better."

Kemal laid back down on the bench and grasped the bar. "Ten this set, Riordan." He did them without effort.

When he was through, I said, "A revolutionary group claimed credit for shooting Turner. Are you tapped into any groups that would know about them?"

Kemal laughed. "At my age? They'd think I was FBI." He went on, saying, "No, I never heard of them. If they were here, I think I would have, unless they're right wing, not left. But I wouldn't be part of them. All I'm after is peaceful coexistence with the whites. And a decent return on four-hundred years of invested sweat."

"Did you know Deborah Greene was dead?" I asked.

"I saw it in the paper. Killed by a burglar. That's a shame," he said, without emotion.

"It was no burglar. I was questioning her that night. Just before she was killed she called me and said she would tell me about Joshua. Who was Joshua, Kemal?"

He didn't answer. He took the bar off the weight rack

and did another ten repetitions, his arms shaking with fatigue. When he finished I asked him again. He closed his eyes, then sat up, smiling.

"Joshua was a prophet of the Hebrew Bible," he said sarcastically. "Made walls fall down with a trumpet. Even made the sun stand still." Kemal took his towel off the bench and draped it around his shoulders, hanging on to the ends. "A trick, by the way, that many have tried and few have accomplished."

"I think you know who killed Turner and Greene," I said angrily.

"Oh, I don't, Riordan. I surely do not. But I can tell you that you're not going to find the answer here."

"He may decide to kill all of you."

"He?"

"Joshua."

"No, Riordan. Not me. I'm not involved." He stood up and said, "I've got to shower before I tighten up. Don't try to press this thing on me, Riordan. It's not my problem." He walked calmly away.

I never saw him again.

CHAPTER 13

Tuesday morning at ten o'clock the Seattle Police and the feds were meeting to go over what they had so far in the Turner case. Vince Ahlberg said I could come if I promised to say nothing stupid. Or better yet, nothing at all.

Somewhere there is a master designer of big-city police headquarters. He—women have better taste—designs the building so that inside it is always six o'clock on a rainy afternoon, no matter if the sun is shining outside. The walls are painted one of two colors, dirty beige or drab olive-green. The floor is always steel-gray linoleum scarred by burn marks. The desks are battered steel-gray with gray formica tops. A few years back they tried to change the design by having some artistically talented prisoners doing County time paint colorful murals on the walls. They had a little press conference to unveil the murals. One of the murals showed the Chief of Police doing some biologically unlikely things with both members of a K-9 unit. After that they stuck with olive drab.

The conference room was full of cops and smoke when I walked in. A short, burly guy dressed in a plastic brown-checked suit walked over. He was half-bald, but compensated with furry eyebrows, a thick mustache, and wide muttonchop sideburns. Underneath the fur he looked familiar. He took his cigarette out of his mouth, stuck the other hand out, and said, "Clyde Dimmick, U.S. Drug Enforcment Assistance Admin . . . Riordan? Is that fucking you, Riordan?"

"Hiya, Dimmy," I replied. "Very long time."

"Ahlberg?" He spun around. "Ahlberg!" he shouted. "What is this clown doing here?"

Ahlberg stepped over. He took one look at Dimmick and a wide smile split his face. "I take it you two know each other," he said to me.

"We've met," I replied.

Dimmick grabbed Vince by the lapels. The cigarette in his mouth jumped up and down, dribbling ashes on his protruding belly. "Listen to me, Ahlberg, you can't have this moron in the meeting. He threw out two-thirds of my goddamn cases when he was with the Boston strike force. The shitheads would come in with their damn lawyers and a half-hour later they'd walk. He'll leak like a fucking sieve on this case. Get him the hell out of here." Vince took both of Dimmick's hands off his suit. Then he looked at me. "Yeah?" he said.

"We used to call him Dimmy," I said, "because he would blow a perfectly decent bust on some unique and creative Fourth-Amendment violation that even the Supreme Court hadn't thought of yet. In the two years I was in Boston he had two partners shot out from under him. He never got scratched. We all wondered what it was he had up his ass. Finally figured it must be a rabbit's foot.''

Dimmick growled and stepped toward me. Ahlberg stepped in his way. Dimmick tried to push. Pushing Ahlberg is like trying to shove a tree. It burns up calories but doesn't get you anywhere.

"Matthew," Vince said forcefully. "Shut up." To Dimmick: "He's the attorney for the victim's family. He stays. Let's get the damn meeting started."

The room had gotten quiet, but the buzz of conversation picked back up again. I walked down to the end of the conference table and pulled up a chair next to a homicide detective named Wechsler, a wire-thin, redheaded guy who chain-smoked Camels and told bad jokes to everybody he came in contact with: victims, suspects, families, judges. Once Wechsler was questioning a twenty-two-year-old kid charged with killing his ten-year-old cousin for no good reason. The kid was a neurotic punk but had seen a lot of TV and was going to tough it out. Wechsler started telling jokes. Jewish jokes. P.R. jokes. Knock-knock jokes. He told his third elephant joke, and the kid cracked. The kid's lawyers took it all the way to the Court of Appeals. The Court agreed that the jokes were very bad but said they didn't amount to an unconstitutional third-degree. After that Wechsler couldn't be stopped. "Hey, Matt," he said, "did you hear about these two very short leprechauns: they go up to the mother superior of a convent—"

"Yes," I said quickly. "What've you got so far?"

"It's mostly shit. But the lieutenant will tell you."

Ahlberg stood up and said, "All right, let's go. Let me recap for everybody who's not up to speed on this. The witness statements from the shooting at the restaurant are all Xeroxed, and each of you has the packet. None of them, including Riordan, the tall guy in the back of the room there, saw very much. The car was a white 1972 Buick Electra, pimped out with stripes and that mirror-film stuff on the windows, which is why nobody could see in. It was stolen four hours before the shooting from a garage at Twentieth and Cherry. State Patrol found it abandoned by the freeway off ramp near Boeing Field. The shooter probably dumped it within minutes. No prints and nothing distinctive in the lab analysis of soil and fibers. The weapon was sure as hell distinctive. An AR-15 Armalite Commando, either the real thing or modified for full automatic fire. Nine rounds fired, we think. Four hit the victim, Stephen Turner. Damn near cut him in half.''

Ahlberg paced at the front of the room, letting his words sink in.

"The victim's family has been talked to. There's one sister, here in town, and four cousins in the area. None of them had any reason to kill him, or knows why anyone else would want to. Turner worked at a computer company called macroprocess. We've talked to the president, named Darwin, and most of the victim's coworkers. Same story. We've checked a list of friends provided by Turner's sister. Most of them were just acquaintances. Turner was pretty much a loner, I guess. Also the same story.''

"As some of you know, Turner was indicted ten years ago for conspiracy, as part of a radical group called the Northwest Nine. They were supposed to have bombed a courthouse and some electric transmission towers, but they were never convicted. We've talked to four members of that group, Mustafa Kemal, George Shields, Kyle Parman, and Diane Olmstead. All denied being involved in any radical activities today. They don't know why Turner might have been picked for a terrorist hit, because he had given up radical activities a long time ago. Nor did they know anything about this new group that's claimed credit, Pacific Liberation Faction."

Ahlberg continued pacing. He started to scratch at the blackboard, then stopped and wiped out the chalk marks with his hand. "There are two things that bother me. One is that this is so obviously a professional attack. The weapon and timing were professional, although it doesn't make sense to hit a guy in front of a restaurant crowd unless you are after media coverage, and that does indicate a terrorist group. The other thing is that a woman named Deborah Greene, a teacher at the University of British Columbia who was once active in the Northwest Nine, was killed up in Vancouver about nine hours after Riordan over there went up to interview her."

Dimmick said, "So, arrest him." Nobody laughed.

"What those two things add up to," Ahlberg said, "is that if this group is for real, they are very damned good. "Any comments?"

A short, calm-looking man stood up, tugged his vest back down over his paunch, and said, "Harmon Broderick, with the Bureau. We're not really sure what we've got here, except we remember Turner and the others from the good old days. The terrorism thing, as we see it, is still worth more checking. Terrorism could be reviving at any time, and they could see the old radicals as targets, given that most have now renounced their old beliefs." He sat back down.

Nobody had anything to say about that. Then Dimmick

stood up. "Clyde Dimmick, DEA. We had the victim, uh, Turner, under surveillance off and on for two months prior to his death. He's a known associate of Daniel Schoen, who's one of the largest distributors of smoke and blow in the Tacoma area."

Wechsler turned his pale bleak eyes to me. "Smoke? and Blow?" he asked.

"He's probably been reading *Rolling Stone* again," I replied.

Dimmick was still going ". . . and in a search of the victim's summer home on Lopez Island, we located better than five ounces of sinsemilla and almost four ounces of high-grade blow. There's no doubt that ties him in as a dealer. Make it very hard to hang a conviction of the killers, but it's almost certainly the Colombians. They are taking over wholesaling on this coast just like they did in Florida. The terrorist thing, we think, is a cover story." Dimmick looked very pleased with himself. Everybody knew the Colombians were tough to stop. He now had a solid reason for failing. No one could blame him. Every bureaucrat's wet dream.

Dimmick sat down. Vince Ahlberg turned his tired stare down the table. "Anybody got any different ideas?"

Wechsler looked over at me. "Should you or I?"

"I'm just an interested citizen," I replied.

Wechsler stood up. "With all due respect to our druggies," he said looking at Dimmick, "did you guys think to check out Turner's background? Or finances? The guy inherited something like two million bucks four years ago. You'd have to deal in pounds of cocaine to turn enough bucks just to match the interest on that kind of money." He took a drag off his cigarette and stubbed it out. "As for Turner's being a friend of Schoen, so what? They'd known each other for fifteen years. Schoen is a shit, no doubt, but Turner was still his friend. As for the drugs, well, maybe you guys just got careless and dropped a few souvenirs during the search."

Dimmick leaned back in his chair. "Your name's what, Wechsler? Let me tell you, Wechsler, I've got twenty years in law enforcement, and I know when I've got the stuff. We got three photographed meetings between Turner and Schoen. Two in parking lots. One in a shopping mall. You go to see your buddies in a shopping mall? Chat about old times there in front of Thom McAn Shoes? And one other thing . . ." Dimmick leaned forward and put both hands flat on the table. "Next time you accuse me of a plant, you'd better do it by telegram. Because if I can reach you, I'm gonna shove your head up your asshole."

Wechsler had his mouth ready to go, but Ahlberg's raspy tenor cut him off. "This isn't productive," he said. "Thank you for coming over. That's it."

Ahlberg stood up, and the meeting crowd filed out. I hung back waiting while Ahlberg poured his fourth or fifth cup of twice-boiled coffee. He liked it that way. He looked up at me and said, "What do you think?"

"I'd go with Wechsler. Turner was not the type to deal. Or use; not much anyway. He probably smoked some social dope. So do I."

"Not with me. But Dimmick has something, Matthew. Those meetings are hard to explain."

"Maybe. Schoen denies having seen Turner at all. Which means he probably did. The bastard would lie for free." I walked over and poured myself another cup of boiled coffee and tasted it. It was bad. "Here's one other fact you need to know, Vince. Henry Cruz came around a few days back to politely suggest that I stay the hell out of this thing. When the only people who knew I was working on it were me, Kate, and your office. Which means you've probably got a leak in your office.''

"Damn it," he said bitterly. "What's Cruz got to do with this?''

"I don't know. But he's in it.''

"Jesus. I don't know which is worse. Terrorism. Or drugs. Or Cruz.''

"Maybe all three.''

"You need a guy to watch your back, Matthew?''

"Thanks. I got one. He's good.''

Ahlberg nodded and said, as if thinking aloud, "You know, I'd like to put some heat on Schoen, maybe see if we can find out why he and Turner were meeting. But he operates out of Pierce County, owns or rents half the county sheriff's department. Dimmick says even he can't put anything together down there.''

"Gotcha," I replied. "A little private-sector pressure on the man would probably get overlooked.''

Ahlberg smiled his first smile of the morning and said, "Something like that.''

CHAPTER 14

George Shields practiced law with his father in a firm called Shields, Hart & Shields. Not a big law firm, but a wealthy one, its practice was mostly devoted to the care and feeding of the local fortunes made in shipping, airplanes, and construction. Their offices, on the forty-ninth story of a bank building with all the architectural merit of a cigar box, were designed to reassure the customers with thick carpets and carved oak paneling. I thought they looked like a cross between a bank and a whorehouse, as such a more than usually honest artistic statement about the practice of law.

I sat in the lobby and watched as Shields came in. He was thirty-six now, not as good-looking as he had been at twenty. A stocky man headed for stout, his features had thickened with age and weight. But when he walked into a room, you could feel his entrance on the air like a change in the weather. He trailed behind him the usual two or three aides that all politicians attract like iron to a magnet. He shooed them away and shook my hand and called me Matt while we walked back to his office.

"How 'bout a sandwich and a beer?" he asked. "I ate lunch in three nursing homes today. Meaning I talked and smiled and sipped some water. Couldn't eat that slop. But you've got to go after the elderly vote."

I said yes to the lunch and added, "Your campaign looks good. You're up sixteen points in the last newspaper poll."

"Yeah," he replied, "but with TV you can lose it so damn fast. That's why you've got to campaign hard. It's a pain. Still, I get a charge out of it. Hundreds of people looking at you, pulling for you, trusting you. It's electric, the feeling you get."

A pretty young clerk brought in a tray of beer and sandwiches. Shields thanked her, and she backed away, smiling. For a minute I was afraid she would curtsy.

"This is about Steve Turner, right?" Shields asked around a mouthful of corned beef.

"Right. I represent his sister, not the estate. She asked me to look into his death when the police investigation got stalled."

"Why hire a lawyer instead of an investigator?"

"I don't know. I used to be a Justice Department investigator and a strike-force prosecutor. If I'm a luxury, I'm one she can afford."

"Can she ever." Shields drained the dregs from one bottle of beer and opened another. "So, why come to me? I hadn't seen Steve in over a year."

"Because I think his killing is connected in some way to the Northwest Nine trial."

Shield's fixed smile fell off his face like a stone.

"Oh, Christ," he said. "Just what I need. A month before the election and you're going to dredge up all that old crap again. Why?"

"Two of the defendants in that trial have been murdered in the last four weeks. That's just too damn much coincidence."

"Oh, come off it, Riordan," he sighed. "There was a terrorist group that took credit for killing Steve. The Liberation Something. Faction."

"And nobody can find them, Shields. Nobody. They've got no known members, no set ideology, no apparent connections with any other groups, old or new. Maybe they come from someplace so new that we don't know where to look. Or maybe they're a front for something else."

"You know, so far I haven't heard anything but a bunch of maybes from you."

"I've got a little more than that, George. I've got two dead peoople, and nobody can figure out who killed them. And I've got a name. I'm looking for someone named Joshua, George. I think you knew him. Who was he?"

He didn't answer the question. He sat back in his wide leather chair, frowning in concentration. "Damn it, this could just kill me. And it's not fair, Riordan. I gave up all that nonsense a long time ago. Intellectually, I worked my way around to libertarianism and market capitalism. Then, when I accepted Jesus, I rejected everything—"

"Yeah," I cut in, fearing a speech, "and you did it beautifully, George. But maybe some of your old comrades are still out there and might be a bit pissed off at your change of heart. Who was this guy Joshua?"

"Look, Riordan, I don't know anybody named Joshua.
"I—oh, hello, Dad."

George Shields II walked into his son's office without
knocking, as if he owned it. He probably did. The elder
Shields was short and broad like his son, but with no trace
of softness. He had a belly like a brick from thirty years of
sit-ups, squash, and a single lunchtime martini at the
athletic club. With his County Mayo nose and balding pink
scalp he looked like a leprechaun. A big, mean, grown-up
leprechaun. He looked at me inquisitively.

"This is Matthew Riordan, Dad. He represents Kate
Warden, Stephen Turner's sister."

Old Shields stuck out a hand. "Pleased to meet you,
Riordan. I hear good things about you. Understand you
really stuck it to Ben Fleishacker in a trial a couple
weeks back."

I shook his hand. "Ben Fleischacker's clients were
guilty of gross negligence," I replied. "That helped a
lot."

"Still, you have to know what the hell to do with judge
and jury, young fellow. And you sure did. What brings
you down here, talking to my boy George?" I glanced at
his boy George. He had a calm, blank look on his face.
But his jaw was clamped shut, hard. I liked him a little
better for that.

To his father, I said, "I'm trying to find out if the
murders of Stephen Turner and Deborah Greene are connected to the Northwest Nine trial."

"Jesus!" he exclaimed. "What's your proof that they
are?"

"I don't have any proof. I've got a reasonable basis for

belief. I'm looking for a man named Joshua. Then I might have some proof."

Shields said, "Does that name mean anything to you, son?"

"Not a thing, Dad," George replied. "I didn't know anyone by that name when I was in school."

The older Shields turned back to me. His eyes glittered like bright stones. He said, "So you see, we can't help you, Mr. Riordan. Now, as you know, my boy's running for Congress. He's got it won, in fact. The only thing that could stop him would be some sort of irresponsible rumor. George was involved in a lot of damn foolishness in the sixties. Most kids were. You probably were yourself. And most grown-ups, like me, overreacted. That's all past now. George has got no connection with it anymore. He's talked to the police. They're satisfied." He leaned forward in his chair. "Now, let me suggest that you conduct yourself as a responsible member of the bar." He smiled coldly. "If one word of your 'investigation' leaks to the press, I will finish you in this town. Finally and completely." Then he added, "You're a good young lawyer, my friend. We need good lawyers. We could send a lot of trial business to you. This investigation you're doing won't last very long. What you need is steady work. We can give you that." He spoke with the calm arrogance of a man long used to power. And he pissed me off.

I said, "I have no intention of hurting George's prospects, Mr. Shields, other than voting for somebody else. Anybody else. But I'm going to pursue this investigation, wherever it goes." I smiled at both of them. "It's kind of ironic. I got the very same offer you two gave me from Henry Cruz. I think that says a lot, don't you?"

I stalked out of the building. I had gotten the last word, but that wasn't worth much. I had no witnesses and no facts. If the Shieldses, father or son, had been a little smarter, they could have seen that I was all out of doors to open. In a few days I would have to tell Kate that there was nothing more I could do.

I went down to the basement garage and got my battered, half-restored MG from the parking attendant. He was a nice kid who said he knew of a good mechanic who worked on English cars on his own time, cheap, and he'd get me the phone number. I pulled my car off to the side of the ramp and waited for him. I was still waiting when George Shields' silver Jaguar flashed by. Shields bounced the car on the sidewalk so hard that sparks flew, ran the red light on Seneca Street, and was gone.

Sometimes it is better to be lucky than good. I cranked the MG over, offered a brief prayer to the pagan gods of English motors, and took off after him.

I caught him on Interstate 5, heading south, dodging nervously through the thickening afternoon traffic. The rush of cars helped as I tried to stay four or five cars back. I had worked with enough cops and read enough books to know how you were supposed to pull a tail, but there is a sizable distance between theory and practice.

Too much distance. Shields got off the interstate near the airport and cut over to Pacific Highway South. I had to concentrate on staying out of sight, yet close enough not to be stranded on the wrong side of a stoplight. I was working so hard at it that I didn't notice that the tailer had become the tailee.

A blue sedan cut hard across my path, and I threw the MG into a braking skid, my rear wheels fishtailing to the left as the sedan nosed me to the right. I had to fight to hold my car on the narrow shoulder and stay out of the ditch. An identical sedan with the same rent-a-car blandness pulled up close behind me. Before I could decide what to do, a tall, thin black man jerked open my passenger door, pointed an ugly snub-nosed .38 revolver at me, and folded himself in.

"Howdy," he said conversationally, a trace of the South in his voice. "Doan do anything stupid, man, an' you'll be okay. Follow the blue car. Doan look around. I'll waste you if I need to." He shifted uncomfortably in the bucket seat. "Man, these cars are small."

I said nothing and drove. The blue sedan led me a couple of miles down Pacific Highway South. When we passed Danny Schoen's nightclub, I looked carefully at the parking lot. George Shield's silver Jaguar was parked in the second row.

It didn't make much sense. If the auto circus boys were there to keep me off Shields, they would never have paraded me past his destination. Unless they didn't care what I saw.

They took me to the sort of grim ramshackle side-of-the-highway motel where you can register by the hour, and if you complain about the cockroaches, the manager will look up from his beer just long enough to hand you a can of Raid. I parked as I was told, behind the motel, away from the highway. The thin black man pulled me out of the car and shoved me against the wall to search me.

"He's clean," he said to the driver of the blue sedan.

"Take him in," the other replied.

The black man and I walked into the motel like old friends, his hand against the small of my back to guide me. I followed him carefully. I knew the gun was in the other hand.

The room he took me to was dark. The shades were tightly drawn, and the only light seeped in from cracks around the windows. A man was sitting in a chair facing me. He was smoking a cigar. I could see him only as a dark silhouette. The cigar end glowed brightly. Then a lamp switched on.

Eddie Bogan sat in the chair.

"Well, hot shit, Eddie," I said. "Nice to see you. For a while there I was worried."

He stood up, frowning. "I'm not taking any shit from you, Riordan," he said. "You've fucked up this time." Then he hit me in the belly.

It was a good punch. I doubled up, gasping. Sour vomit exploded from my mouth. A wave of nausea dropped me to my knees.

I saw the kick coming and dodged and took most of it on my shoulder. I couldn't dodge the knee that followed. It caught me high on the cheekbone, and I fell backward in a bright mist of pain.

"Get him up," Eddie Bogan said. He sounded very far away.

Bogan's helpers dragged me to my feet. They propped me up, swaying. Bogan slapped me once, then again. Blood seeped into my mouth.

"Riordan?" he said, slapping me again, getting his weight behind each blow. "You paying attention, Riordan? Then, listen up. You don't bother Danny and me again, Riordan. You don't come into our place, you don't ask questions, and whatever the hell you're doing, you drop it." My head rocked as he slapped me again. He had something in his hand, and it cut me. Blood filled my eyes, and I was blind behind a dark-red curtain.

I don't remember much of the rest of it. Something broke in my chest, and I started having trouble breathing. The last thing I do remember, just before I blacked out, is a soft commanding voice saying "That's enough."

The voice belonged to Henry Cruz.

CHAPTER 15

By Saturday, four days later, I was very nearly a well man. The total damage was a mild concussion and three broken ribs, amounting to a two-day headache and some chest pain that truly did hurt only when I laughed. This is not to run down the quality of the beating that I got. Nothing hurts like a professional beating, and Bogan and his two hitters had given me bruises in places where a tattoo artist couldn't go. But Cruz was behind it, and he had a code that called for a maximum of message and a minimum of really serious damage.

I also had good doctoring. Kate had insisted that I stay with her and I had, gladly. She told me jokes and read to me and stayed with me at night. She joined me in the tub for long soaks to take some of the stiffness out of my bruises. We laughed like children when the soaking turned into something much more fun. I had been living alone for a long time, and I had grown used to the silences. Usually

I foung it hard to accept the thousand small changes that living with someone else brings to your life. This time it wasn't hard at all.

I was down at my office, reading the mail and thinking about a late lunch, when Bernstein came in. He collapsed into a chair with a shot of bourbon and lit a Camel. He looked at me with a mournful expression on his face. "I never thought it could happen," he muttered, shaking his head. .

"What? What happened?" I asked, concerned. Bernstein normally has the ego of a surgeon who climbs mountains.

"I have been sitting in a topless bar for three-and-a-half days now. Best surveillance duty I ever drew, drinking my own bourbon and watching the little darlings do their thing. And you know what? I got tired of it. Unlimited teenage T and A, and I got tired of it." He grunted irritably and swallowed more whiskey.

"Advancing age," I said. "You'll probably be impotent next. Senility and death to follow."

He said, "Fuck you, Matthew" with considerable conviction.

"So, what did you find out? Aside from the fact you may be finally getting through adolescence."

"Our boy Danny is dealing, all right. Definitely coke, probably some grass, too. Caters strictly to the wholesale trade. He's so fucking dumb he moves it right out of that place of his. Or else he's protected."

"Probably protected. He's connected to Henry Cruz. Cruz leases the county law down there." I got a can of beer from my small office refrigerator and cut a finger opening the pop top, silently cursing the inventor of the damned things. "But the protection can't hold up forever. Cruz can't control the feds, not all of them, anyway. Cruz must have some other reason to prop Schoen up. Maybe George Shields is involved, too."

Bernstein looked thoughtful. "He's the politician you were following out there? You know, he never showed up in the bar. Meaning he was there seeing Danny, not scratching a boyhood fantasy or two. So you've scared him and Schoen into making a connection, and both of them had recently seen Turner. I say we've got something." He drained the last of his whiskey and set the glass on my desk.

"Maybe," I admitted, "but we still don't know what the hell it means. I think the time has come to twist Danny a little. Too bad beating him up wouldn't work."

"No. And he'll just hire some more local talent to return the favor. As you found out."

I rubbed my sore ribs and said nothing. The bruises on my belly had just begun to turn yellow. Bernstein is sometimes right too often.

"But I think I might have an angle," he said, smiling with satisfaction and going for a beer.

"So, give," I replied.

"He's making a buy tonight."

"Why? Wouldn't he get his product through Cruz?"

"Usually. But apparently Cruz has been dry. They're tapping another source."

"Not bad," I said. "A citizen's arrest might do good things for his memory and speaking ability. How'd you find out?"

"Bribery," he said cheerfully. "A young lady named Maggie who dances there has two hundred bucks and a gram of coke she didn't have to fuck anybody for. Put it on your expense account. I'm going to.''

"Wonderful," I said. "Maybe I can hide you under miscellaneous. Or mileage. Bribes are not tax deductible, Bernstein. When and where?"

"She knew it was tonight, but she doesn't know where. She said the bouncer would know. Eddie Bogan. He's not working this afternoon."

I got up from my chair. Slowly. The ribs were healing, but my body was still tight as a clenched fist from the bruises. I walked over to the safe and took out a Smith & Wesson .357, a gun with no known virtues except for the fact that it scares people badly and can knock out a sperm whale at thirty feet. I squirmed into a woven leather shoulder rig and holstered the gun. I don't much like wearing guns or using them. But I was going after Eddie Bogan, and I wasn't gonna do it as Christian charity on the hoof.

Eddie Bogan lived hard by the Highway 99 airport strip, in one of those tired stucco apartment houses that always looks like somebody just died there. Bernstein and I parked our nondescript rented Ford sedan in a used-car lot on the highway two blocks away.

"Let's hope they don't sell it," I said.

"I hope they do. Never saw anything more worthless than a Ford," Bernstein grumbled.

"Your Dodge half-ton four-by-four pickup, bright orange with the stainless steel pig mounted as a hood ornament, does tend to get noticed down here in the city."

"Don't want to get shot at during elk season," he exlained.

"Oh, yeah, we get a lot of those elk around here."

"Shut up. We're here."

The apartment lobby was small and dirty and maybe furnished from bankruptcy sales. The once-white walls had been stained by water and worse. The rust-colored carpet was ripped and burned from being used as an ashtray. Bogan's name was on the mail slot that read B-3. The basement. "T and A must not pay all that well," Bernstein commented.

"I suspect Eddie's in it for the fringe benefits. Rapine and pillage."

We paused in the corridor outside Bogan's apartment. His door was made of pressboard and glue, and sound carried through it like it was air. Inside the apartment, a radio played Duran Duran. There was also a sound of heavy breathing, a slap of metal, and a rhythmic grunting. Bernstein looked at me, an amused question in his eyes.

"Think we caught him at a bad time?" he asked.

I shrugged my shoulders and pointed to the door. Bernstein counted silently to three, mouthing the numbers, and kicked in the door.

I went through in a low, scrambling crouch, the big gun ready. None of the dramatics were necessary.

Eddie Bogan lay on his back on a plastic exercise bench. His arms were half extended, pushing up a hundred-pound barbell. His mouth was slack with surprise, and his eyes were sick. I stuck the muzzle of the .357 in his ear. And smiled.

"Hello, Eddie," I said quietly. "Move, and the walls are gonna need repainting."

He nodded his head a fraction of an inch, just enough to show he'd been listening. He started to put the barbell back on its rack. "No, Eddie," I said, "keep it up. Let's see how strong you are without those two gorillas around to help you with your hitting."

He held up the barbell. His arms began to shake with fatigue. Dressed up he looked big and tough. In his shorts he was just another thirty-five-year-old guy with a beer gut and a double chin.

I said, "We hear Danny's got a deal doing down tonight, Eddie. When, where, and who's going with him on the buy for cover? You?"

"Buy? I don't know what you're talking about, man." Bogan's voice had a lot of strain in it, but he kept it quiet. He had some balls on him after all.

"Sure you do, Eddie. You see enough snow going through that place to get a job with the weather bureau."

His whole body was shaking now, but he shook his head. "You're crazy, man."

Bernstein shook his head and let out a disgusted snort. "Step back," he said to me. He walked up behind Bogan's head, put one hand on the poised barbell, and sent it crashing down on Bogan's chest.

Eddie Bogan screamed. Not a high feminine scream like you hear in the movies. It was a low hissing gurgling scream, with genuine pain in it. Bernstein changed his grip on the bar and took the weight off Bogan, just enough so he could breathe. Bernstein's voice got very soft. He said, "Listen to me very carefully, Eddie. You think you can play games with me, you're wrong. Riordan here is a nice guy, but I'm not. You're going to talk to me, or I'm going to kill you. The next time this bar comes down on your throat. Your larynx will be crushed, and it'll take about five minutes for you to strangle yourself. And the cops'll think you're just another dumb weekend jock who lost his grip on a sweaty barbell.''

Bernstein lifted the bar with one hand. Eddie Bogan sobbed quietly.

"Oh, Christ," he said, "they'll kill me."

"Them later, Eddie," Bernstein replied. "Me now."

"Please. Okay." Bogan sprawled on the bench, his arms quivering with fatigue as they dragged on the floor. Oily sweat poured from his skin.

Bernstein set the barbell back on the weight rack. "Talk to me," he demanded.

Bogan sat up, disoriented. He rubbed his arms, and the long ropy muscles, blurred by fat, jumped and twitched.

"Danny's making a buy tonight, like you said," Bogan whispered. "It'll be in Seattle, down on Western under the Pike Market. Danny's got a thing about not getting blown away in a rip-off, so he takes the chance to meet in cars, out in the open."

"What's Danny buying?" I asked.

"Coke. Maybe a little Thai stick."

"Why isn't he getting it through Cruz?"

"Regular source dried out. And I think Cruz wants to get out of importing."

I looked at Bernstein. "What do you think?" I asked.

He shrugged. "Scumbag here might just be telling the truth. If Cruz is established, he'll lay off the high-risk stuff, leave it for someone else. They say service industries are the wave of the future."

I turned back to Bogan. "What time? And what kind of car will Danny be driving?"

"Around ten, ten-thirty. When the bars are full. I don't

know the car. It'll be some kind of rented sedan. American. Plain."

"Right. Who's Danny got to provide cover? You?"

"Not this time. Usually it'd be me, but Danny's got somebody else. He won't tell me who he is, or anything. But he must be very heavy and very expensive."

"Why?"

"This guy comes straight from Cruz, man." Eddie Bogan looked me over. He said, "Ever since you came around, Riordan, Danny's been very uptight. And when Danny's nervous he wants the very best."

Bernstein looked at me, and I shrugged. We had squeezed Bogan dry. Bernstein turned to go. Bogan called out after him.

"Hey, hang on, man. You got to tie me up."

"What the hell for?" Bernstein asked.

"If you don't," Bogan replied, "I gotta call Danny. And then I gotta go after you."

Bernstein stared, dumbfounded. Then he sighed.

"Eddie, you've seen too many movies," he said. "The situation is simple. Watch my lips. If you call Schoen, I will shoot you. If you come after us, I will shoot you. Probably several times."

Bogan looked down at the ground. He said, "I know all that, man. Both of you are better than me. But I'd have to try."

"Why?" I asked.

"Because it's my job, Riordan. It's what I signed on for."

"Okay," I said to Bernstein. "Tie him up."

"There's some rope in the bedroom closet," Bogan offered.

Bernstein came back with the rope. He looked at both of us darkly.

"Easier to kill him," he muttered.

Bogan looked at me. "Is he always this mean?" he asked.

"I've seen him worse," I replied.

"Holy shit," he said, reverently.

He added, "Riordan? The other day? No hard feelings, right? That was just business."

I started to tell him to fuck off, but I held back and looked around his apartment. A worn rust-plaid couch sagged against a wall like a fat man out of breath. A broken coffee table teetered on taped-up legs. The remains of two or three take-out meals were scattered around the room. Eddie Bogan would have troubles enough until the day when life finally ran over him for the last time.

"Eddie," I said finally, "you are a shit, but you are a loyal shit. If you get into trouble I can help you with, I will."

He started to smile, and I pistol-whipped him across the face. "Just one thing, Eddie," I said. "Don't ever laugh when you're handing out a beating. It ain't funny."

He nodded. His right eye began to swell even before Bernstein finished tying him up.

CHAPTER 16

"That's it," Bernstein said. "It's going down."

We were standing on an open deck behind a long corridor lined with produce stalls in the Pike Place Market, the largest surviving urban farmer's market in the country. The Market is the soul of Seattle, lovingly preserved, yet not an antique. During the day it is a bright swirl of people and food and crafts. This night it was empty. Sounds creaked and chattered hollowly through it, as though the ghost of Mark Tobey himself were walking through the empty stalls.

I looked down at Danny Schoen's car, parked on Western, down the hill from the Market. A second car had pulled up behind it. A man with a briefcase walked up to Schoen's car and got in.

"Let's go," I said.

We ran down the Pike Place stairs. When we got to the bottom, Bernstein stopped and pulled me into a doorway.

"Where's his backup?" he hissed.

"I don't know. Maybe he hasn't got any."

"Why would Eddie lie?" he asked. "We should have been able to find him. I don't like this."

"This is it, Bernstein. We've got to go with it. It's our only chance to squeeze Schoen."

"I still don't like it," he insisted.

We waited. Within minutes the second man walked back to his car and drove away. We ran to Schoen's car, one of us on each side. Bernstein ripped open the driver's door and stuck his big .45 automatic in Danny Schoen's face.

"Hi there," he said.

I slid into the car from the passenger side.

"Evening, Danny," I said conversationally. A drug-testing kit was on the seat. Next to it was a plastic package the size of two books. I slit open the plastic and pinched off some white powder and rubbed it on my gums. They tingled pleasantly. Cocaine. "Tasty," I said. "Dentists should use this stuff."

Danny Schoen sat stiffly behind the wheel. "You're cute, Riordan," he said tightly. "Very cute. Beating you up wasn't enough. Okay. You'll be dead within the hour."

"Don't think so, Danny. You see, there isn't anybody out there. I think you've been forsaken, pal. Move over so my friend can get in."

Bernstein squeezed behind the wheel and shut the door. He doesn't just get into cars, he puts them on.

"What we've got here, Danny," I explained, "is your basic citizen's arrest for felony narcotics possession. With intent to traffic, I should think. Don't get any ideas about running. Citizens in this state are authorized to use deadly force to stop you fleeing felons.''

"What the fuck do you want, Riordan?'' he asked tiredly.

"I want to know about you and Turner and Shields, Danny. You got photographed talking to Turner twice in the last two months. You put all that coke in his apartment. Why? Where does Shields fit into this? He was on his way to your club when your hired help jumped me.''

"Fuck you.''

Bernstein twisted around and casually punched Schoen in the face.

"And one other thing,'' I added. "Who is Joshua?''

Schoen shook his head and laughed, groggily. Blood leaked from his mouth. "You know, Riordan, you are so far off base on this Joshua thing you might as well be in Alaska. You don't know what you're talking about.''

"Educate me.''

"Why?''

"Talk to me and you walk away from this with the goods,'' I answered. "Stay quiet and you buy long prison time.''

Schoen thought it over, his face like stone in the dark.

"Not good enough,'' he said finally. "You get nothing, Riordan. Not from me.''

"Let's go,'' Bernstein said. "I don't like sitting here. You want to take his car?''

"Listen to your friend, Riordan,'' Schoen cut in. "You're dead down here.''

"No. Wait.'' Try to deal, I told myself. Think like a prosecutor. "Listen, Danny. You tell me about Turner and Shields, I'll do a deal for you. Immunity for whatever ties you into this thing. Relocation, if you want it. I was with the feds once, Danny. I know how to pull it off for you."

He laughed in my face. "You're holding air, Riordan. This thing is buried so deep you'll never find it. I said no to Turner. I'm saying no to you."

"You said no to Turner?" I asked, confused. "No to what?"

"Guess, Riordan."

"Come on, Matthew," Bernstein cut in insistently. "We're all out of time. Do we take the car?"

"No. Leave it. Let's take Schoen out on the street and call the cops. I'll take the stuff. You watch the little sleazebag."

I gathered up the coke and the testing kit and started to get out of the car. I was half-in, half-out when Schoen jumped. He was rat-quick. He hit me low in the back and, off-balance, I fell. The coke hit the pavement, and the plastic wrapping split open, spilling the white powder in the street.

Schoen ran for the stairs that led up the hill, into the Market. Bernstein jumped out of the car after him. He hesitated at the pile of coke.

"Just a sample," he said.

"Screw it. Move!" I yelled, getting to my feet.

We chased him up the stairs. I was still stiff from the beating and could hardly run. After the first three flights my legs got heavy and my ribs burned, but I was in better shape than Schoen and gained on him.

He tried cutting into the lower levels of the Market, but the gates were locked. They rattled as he yanked on them desperately. I nearly caught him on the last landing, but I slipped on the wet pavement and fell heavily, sweating and cursing. He gained ground.

I stopped at the top of the stairs beneath the neon-lit Public Market sign. Pike Place curves in front of the Market there, and the corridors of produce stalls and shops split in two directions. Both corridors are locked at night. Schoen had no place to go but the street. I waited.

Seconds later he came out from under the tables at a fishmonger's stall and ran for it. When he reached the street, he stopped. "Raines!" he shouted.

There was no answer. Schoen spun around, almost dancing in frustration.

"Raines!" he shouted again. "Goddammit, Raines!"

Suddenly the Market lights flared on, spotlighting Schoen in the center of the street. Automatic rifle fire burst out from the stalls. Schoen was blown back as the bullets hit him, staggering in hideous dance, like a marionette. When the bullets stopped, Danny Schoen lay like a torn-up rag doll in the street.

Running footsteps trailed away into the Market.

Sirens started in the distance.

Bernstein and I dropped our guns and stepped out into the street to wait for the cops.

On cue, it began to rain.

Bernstein and I waited in the back of a patrol car for the half hour it took Vince Ahlberg to get down to the Market. When he got to the scene, he walked over to what was left of Danny Schoen and lifted the tarpaulin. He stood over the body and looked down. Then he casually dropped the tarpaulin, the way you would on a pile of leaves. Not much of a eulogy.

When he talked to us, he spoke softly, but I could feel his anger rising—distantly, like a summer thunderstorm away on the plains.

"Talk to me," he said. "I'm listening."

"We got a tip that Schoen was going to make a buy down here," I said. "His source had dried up, and he was going to market."

"How'd you get the tip?" Ahlberg asked.

"Threatened to kill a guy," Bernstein replied casually.

"Jesus. I don't think I want to know. Why'd you end up here?"

"The deal was going down on Western," I said. "We caught Schoen while he was shopping. He broke from us while we were taking him out. By the way, the coke's still down on the street down there. You better pick it up before it attracts every Porsche for miles around."

Ahlberg gestured to one of the patrolmen. I told him what to look for, and he left.

"Keep going," Ahlberg said.

"We chased him up the stairs into the Market. He tried to duck into the producue stalls, but the gates were shut. He ran into the street, shouting for his backup. I forget the name."

"Raines," Bernstein said tensely.

"What?" Ahlberg asked.

"The name was Raines," I explained.

"He was standing in the street when the lights came up. It looked like a spotlight was on him. Then he was shot."

"By who?" Ahlberg demanded.

"Christ," Bernstein exploded, "you're dumb even for a cop. By his backup, asshole. The backup probably had orders from Cruz to take Schoen out if the deal went sour.''

Ahlberg and Bernstein glared at each other for a full ten seconds. Then Ahlberg said, "Keep him here, Riordan. We're not through." He ground out the words.

Ahlberg walked away. Bernstein and I stood under the roof of the Market, out of the rain. We smoked and waited. Bernstein looked nervous, a condition I'd thought was as likely as pregnancy for him. He dropped his cigarette and said, "I know that name from somewhere. Raines."

"Good or bad?"

"Not good. Not good at all."

Ahlberg came back and said, "You can go. Statements in my office at noon tomorrow. The next time you get a tip, don't fuck it up. Call me." He looked at the medics loading Schoen into an ambulance. He shook his head. "Amateur night." He left.

We walked to a bar a couple of blocks away. It was a singles bar, all pastels and bleached oak and desperation. We had one drink. I knew if I had more than that, I would not stop.

I called Kate to come down and pick me up. Bernstein sat quietly at the bar, preoccupied.

"What's your plan?" I asked.

"I'm going to sit here and have about five more drinks," he said tiredly, pushing his hair back with both hands. "Then, it being Saturday night, I'm going to get lucky. Tomorrow I'm going to get up late and check on a few things."

"Like what?"

"Like Raines. Take off. Your lady will be waiting." He

hesitated. "Matthew, stay at her house tonight and tomorrow. Yours is in a pretty lonely place."

I walked out of the bar and waited for Kate on the street. It was a warm night. The rain had turned soft. It was a fine night, a night that called for saxophones and champagne and laughter, a night for making love until three o'clock in the morning and falling asleep in your lover's arms.

Kate drove me to her home and sat up with me, watching the sky and the dark waters of the sound until we finally fell asleep sometime after dawn.

CHAPTER 17

On Monday morning, nearly three weeks after her brother had been killed, Kate and I had breakfast at the Athenian Inn in the Pike Place Market to talk about whether she should keep pushing the investigation. We took a booth on the second-story mezzanine, ordered Bloody Marys, and looked out the windows at the rain squalls scudding in across Elliot Bay.

"I talked to Vince Ahlberg again this morning," I began. "He seems convinced that Steve's killing was drug-related, just like Danny Schoen's."

"I don't believe that," Kate replied. "Steve was not dealing."

"I'm not saying you're wrong. But he had some kind of recent connection to Schoen. They weren't friends. That makes those meetings they had hard to explain."

"I know," she said, eyes downcast. "What will the police do now?"

"Ahlberg says he's not going to close it, But he'll treat it more like a drug investigation. They'll put the word out to their street sources that they're after the shooter who took out Schoen. If they get him, they'll figure they've got your brother's killer, too."

"And if they're wrong," she said bitterly, "they won't find Steve's killer."

"Probably not."

She reached across the table and took my hand. Her eyes searched mine. "Matthew, tell me honestly. Do you think Ahlberg's wrong?"

"Yes. The drug theory leaves out Deborah Greene. I don't believe that crap that she was killed by a burglar. Cops are good at solving killings like that. The Victoria Police should have found the burglar by now. And there's the timing. I don't believe in coincidences. Not ones that big." I sighed. "But I don't know where that gets us. We're running out of leads. Fast."

"What's left?"

"There're a couple of people who worked with your brother at Target Zero, the antinuclear group, that I haven't talked to. One of them called me yesterday after the papers put our names in the Schoen story."

"How do you know they have any information?"

"You don't, Kate," I said, smiling and pulling on my coat. "You just keep asking questions until somebody slips up and tells you the truth out of sheer exhaustion."

She pulled on her coat and said, "I'm coming, too. It's about time I got involved in what I've started."

"I don't like that."

"For Christ's sake, Matthew, don't patronize me. I'm not fragile. I'm not going to break."

138

"It's not that. It's just not a good idea to get personally involved."

She turned her crooked smile on me. "Oh, come *off* it, Riordan," she said. "You've been shot at, threatened, beat up, and rousted by the cops. That's not personal?"

"Good point. It's personal."

"Damned right. Let's go."

Bill Schiffman and Jenny Greenberg had worked with Turner at macroprocess as well as at Target Zero. Schiffman didn't want to talk on the phone, so Kate and I drove across Lake Washington on one of the floating bridges that spans the Lake to meet them at their suburban office, hoping against reason that they might give us some new piece of the puzzle that could keep us going.

They met us in the company cafeteria, two good and earnestly liberal people with graying long hair and worn woolen clothes. The sort of people, bless them, who still do macramé and organic baking and holistic medicine. We had coffee. They had herb tea. I liked Bill and Jenny very much, but I was afraid somebody would come along at any moment and put them, like Doonesbury says, in the Smithsonian.

Jenny Greenberg cleared her throat nervously and said, "We really don't know why Steve was killed, Mr. Riordan. We just—well, he told us something that seemed strange, and we thought you should know."

I said, "This is my client, Kate Warden, Steve's sister. She wants to know the truth about why Steve was killed. Please don't be afraid to tell us everything, even if you think it makes Steve look bad."

"About four months ago," Bill Schiffman began nervously, clearing his throat, "we were protesting the arrival of the White Train, that train that transports nuclear bombs to the Trident submarine base over at Bangor on the Hood Canal. It was a peaceful demonstration, but we were trespassing on government property, trying to block the train, so we were arrested. We expected that, of course. Anyway, there was a screwup in getting the money for bail, and we spent most of the night in jail in Bremerton.''

He paused, then went on. ''We got into kind of a discussion. One of those 'why are we here and where are we going' ones. Most of us had been active in the antiwar movement years ago, and we talked about that. Steve was very bitter. He thought we'd accomplished nothing. 'We've gone from Nixon to Reagan,' he said, and the arms race makes Vietnam look like a sideshow. He compared us all to the *narodniki*.''

''The what?'' I asked.

''They were nineteenth-century Russian anarchists,'' Jenny explained. ''Very much upper-class spoiled children.''

''Well, that made a lot of people mad,'' Bill continued. ''They reminded Steve he'd been the well-known sixties rich-kid revolutionary, on TV half of the time, and what had he accomplished? There was some truth in that, and Steve knew it. I think it hurt him pretty bad. He didn't say a word. Finally he said there was one thing he could still do, to shut down nuclear power.''

''What the hell did he mean?'' I asked.

''We never found out. He never said anything else about it. I asked him about it a couple of weeks later, here at work. He just smiled and told me to be patient, he was working on it.''

I was confused and disappointed. It must have shown, because Schiffman stood up and said, ''It's probably nothing, Mr. Riordan. Look, we didn't know what to do. I guess we thought it might be important. Sorry."

Kate smiled and embraced them as they stood to go. "Thank you," she said warmly. "We just don't know what it means. It could mean a lot."

"By the way," I added as we were leaving, "what kinds of things was Steve working on here in the past few months?"

Schiffman looked surprised. "Didn't you talk to Tom Darwin?"

"Sure, but we didn't go into detail."

"Steve was working real closely with Tom, designing custom financial programs. He was doing a little of his education work, but not much. Didn't have time. The financial work is really huge."

Kate and I thanked them again and walked out through a softly lit hallway with pale-rose walls and bleached oak floors.

"Stylish," she murmured. "Thought about redecorating your own office?"

"Pardon me while I check my boots for cowshit and my hair for hay," I replied.

As we reached the reception area a very angry Thomas Darwin stalked up to us.

"What the hell are you doing here, Riordan?" he asked tensely. "I thought we had an understanding about your poking around here without permission. If you screw up our public offering, we're going to sue you."

"I'm not here about your precious company, Darwin, and I don't give a damn about the megabucks you're going to make going public." I said coldly. "I'm here to talk to some people who worked with Turner in Target Zero.

Relax. They didn't know a goddamned thing, either.'' I gestured toward Kate and added, ''This is Mrs. Warden, Turner's sister. I'm sure she's touched by your concern for your late colleague and friend. Now get the hell out of our way.''

I stormed past him, half dragging Kate out of the building with me. We got in the car, and I sat silently behind the wheel for a minute, composing myself.

''What was that all about?'' Kate asked.

''Misanthropy,'' I replied. ''More simply, he just pisses me off.''

''Why?''

''He's worried that your brother's death is going to make his company look bad when they sell stock in a few weeks. That would hold down the price. Then he'd be worth only ten million instead of twenty.'' I shook my head. ''He's so fucking typical of our generation, Kate. He's so goddamned self-centered that he doesn't care if a friend's murder is solved, so long as it doesn't affect him. Look at us, all of us baby-boom kids. When we were against the War, the War was everything. When we did drugs, drugs were everything. When we got into sex, sex was everything. Now we are into money and power. And they are everything. Ordinary people had damn well better stand to one side.''

I tried to let the anger wash out of me as I called my office for messages. Bernstein had called and left a number for me. I called and let it ring. Bernstein picked it up on the fifth or sixth ring.

''Matthew?'' he said, his voice flat, its usual sardonic edge gone.

''Yeah. Where you been, man?''

"Working. Get your ass down here." He gave me an address on Military road, south of the city.

"What the hell is that address?" I asked.

"It's an industrial park. When you get here, come to the warehouse. Bay 23."

"Kate's with me."

He hesitated, then said, "Bring her with. She needs to know this. Now move." He hung up.

Bernstein was waiting for us in a low concrete block warehouse that squatted in the far corner of a small south-end industrial park. I pulled my car up to a blue garage-type door that had the numeral 23 painted on it in red. We waited, the motor running. A man in a blue raincoat and snap-brimmed hat stepped out from a side door. He looked us over carefully. I looked him over carefully. I hadn't seen a snap-brim in years. The man gestured, the garage door rose, and we went in.

"Who are these guys?" Kate murmured.

"Your tax dollars at work, I think."

I parked inside, next to a Cadillac sedan. We got out and looked around. We were in an ordinary high-ceilinged concrete warehouse bay, empty except for a table, chairs, and a portable movie screen set up against the far wall. Bernstein sat on the table, smoking a cigarette and talking to a tall, thin man in a gray pin-striped suit.

The tall man wasn't old, maybe late thirties or early forties. He did not look as if he was having a good time. He looked us over, his angular, bony face filled with disdain.

" 'Bout time," Bernstein said, standing up and flipping his cigarette away. He nodded to Kate. "Matthew, Katherine, this is—"

143

"No names," the thin man cut in.

"Bullshit," Bernstein replied scornfully. "This is Arthur H. Case, the third or the fourth, I forget which. He is the Deputy Director for Administration, United States Central Intelligence Agency."

How do you do? seemed out of place. I said, "So?"

"Artie here is an old friend of mine, Matthew," Bernstein explained sarcastically. "We trained together, back in '67. Artie stayed on with the old CI of A, did real well for himself, climbing the ranks. But he's got this problem. You see, one of his first assignments was to be staff ramrod on an old Frank Hazelton program called Chaos. Remember?"

"I remember," I answered. "Chaos and Cointelpro. CIA and FBI. Domestic spying. Preachers, teachers, kids, vets."

Bernstein smiled and said, "And United States senators. See, Artie, I told you my friend was smart."

"I told you to stop calling me that," Case said nasally.

"Fuck you," Bernstein snapped. "Now we come up to 1975. The Rockefeller Commission starts investigating domestic spying. Artie's called to testify. They ask him, did Creeps in Action ever spy on U.S. Senators? And what does Artie, a gentleman from Choate and Harvard, Harvard Law '66, do?"

I looked at Case. He had a pained look on his face. "He perjures himself," I replied.

"Correct," Bernstein beamed. "Now, here's where our story becomes just a little sinister. There's a new commission staff lawyer, named Hodges, and she doesn't believe Artie's fake gentleman routine. She starts to dig through the CIA records. She gets closer and closer. And all Artie can think is, no more career, no more golf at Burning

Tree, no big fat law firm partnership at three-hundred grand a year when he leaves the Company. He thinks about Danford Prison, where Judge Sirica has just sent a shitload of lawyers from the Watergate case. He thinks nobody would buy his memoirs, which is correct, since unlike Gordon Liddy he's got nothing to say and he's not very interesting, anyway, having been laid maybe two, three times in his entire life."

Bernstein looked at Case with as much savagery as I'd ever seen in him. He said softly, with an edge of real hate, "The next thing you know Hodges comes down with what looks like appendicitis. She gets taken to a D.C. surgeon who's on a Company retainer. There are complications. And she dies."

The room was stone-silent. I looked at Kate. She was white but said nothing. She was tough. It is a hard thing finding out that some nightmares are real.

Bernstein lit another cigarette and blew a gray fog of smoke. "And that is why Artie is here to help us today. Because I can prove it."

Case looked at Bernstein with pure venom. At least they felt the same way about each other. "Let's get this over with," he said shortly. He walked stiffly over to a slide projector and switched it on, training its beam on the screen hung on the wall. The man in the snap-brim at the door dimmed the lights. The first slide clicked into view.

A blond man with a square, blunt face on top of a square, hard body filled the screen. He wore only swim trunks and a deep-water tan as he dribbled a soccer ball on a beach. The photo was fairly good but fuzzy at the edges, as though taken from a long way off with a powerful telephoto lens.

Case gestured at the screen. "Robert Michael Edward Raines," he said. "South African. English family but Afrikaner on his mother's side. He was a captain in their counterinsurgency forces for four years. He was cashiered for corruption."

"And what does he do now?" I asked stupidly.

"Why, he's a killer, Mr. Riordan," Case said with mock sincerity. "A very good one. Free-lance. The Israelis found and trained him and used him in Africa and Egypt in the early seventies, but he's worked for himself since about 1977. This is a list." Case flipped to another slide. A list of names and dates and places filled the screen. I recognized a few of the names—a U.N. Undersecretary-General, a Saudi air-force commander, a South Florida drug dealer—from newspaper obituaries. But it was the list of places that frightened me. Raines hadn't just worked in Addis Ababa and Bahrain and Zurich. He'd also been in Cleveland. Miami. San Jose.

And now here.

"Are you sure he's here?" I asked.

"We're not sure of anything, Riordan. Raines lives in Mexico, a villa at Cozumel." A third slide clicked into place, showing a small stone house shaded by palms. "We have a part-timer in the area who watches the house. Raines left four weeks ago. We haven't been able to trace where."

"Have you told the FBI?"

"Of course. But there are no warrants out for him. Bernstein told them your story. They frankly did not believe him, which is usually the right thing to do. So, they have no interest."

"Does he prefer any particular weapons?"

"Oh, whatever is handy will do for him. He does use a machine pistol very well. Good marksman."

"What about his domestic connections? Does he work for any particular group?"

"Not that the FBI can tell," Bernstein interjected. "But he's worked for some of the major crime syndicates, anyway. Take a look at that list of names."

"I see that." I turned back to Case. "So, what are you going to do to try and find him?"

Case laughed, a small shallow sound in the big room. "Do?" he asked rhetorically. "I'm not going to do anything, Riordan. The CIA doesn't operate domestically anymore. I don't have anyone in place to look for Raines, even if I wanted to. And I don't. I'm on his side. He could solve a problem for me." He smiled coldly. "With any luck at all he'll kill all three of you." Case walked calmly back to his car and got in. The man in the snap-brim started the car. It rumbled hollowly in the empty room. When the door rose, it backed away and was gone.

I watched it go, running my hand nervously against the edge of the table. When I noticed what I was doing, I stopped.

"What do we do now?" I asked Bernstein.

He walked over to Kate as she stood stiffly by the table. He hesitated, then took her gently in his arms and held her. He looked at me over her shoulder.

"Worry," he replied.

CHAPTER 18

Tuesday was the worst day. The very worst day.

Kyle Parman, like many practicing alcoholics, hadn't slept well Monday night. Around three in the morning he left his apartment to go back to his shop. He was restoring an old car, a lovely gray 1963 Jaguar Mark III Saloon. Like most British cars, Jags are a triumph of whimsy over practical engineering, and I think Kyle liked that.

Mustafa Kemal had risen at five to run in Seward Park along the path that traces the southwest shore of Lake Washington. He ran before light because prayers were required at dawn. Kemal wasn't a devout Muslim, but he attended morning prayers because he liked the discipline of body, followed by the discipline of mind.

By dawn both of them were dead.

Kyle Parman's throat had been cut as he leaned into the engine bay of his Jag. Mustafa Kemal had been shot twice, once in the chest, once in the head, to make sure. The shooter had left him on the path beside the lake.

Vincent Ahlberg called me at my office at eight-thirty that morning to give me the news. He added that now they were taking Raines seriously as a suspect, but they hadn't found him. He asked what, if anything, we had found out over the past few days. I told him what little I'd learned from talking to Parman and Kemal. He swore and promised me a grand jury if I was holding out on him and hung up.

Kate and Bernstein and I spent the rest of the morning in my office, waiting, not knowing what we were waiting for. We had no more leads and no more ideas, not even crazy ones. Bernstein and I went over everything we'd done, trying to find something we'd overlooked. We didn't. Our thinking was as garbled as radio waves broken by static.

By ten-thirty or so the press had figured out that Kemal and Parman had been members of the Northwest Nine like Turner. They kept calling for Kate, and I kept yelling no comment at them over the phone until a TV crew showed up outside my office door. Then I sent Bernstein out to reason with them. He threw about ten grand worth of television equipment down three flights of stairs and returned, momentarily satisfied.

I was worried about Kate. She had fought back from the despair after her brother's death, like a swimmer coming back from a deep dive into dark water, pulling herself out with strong strokes. I watched her hard-won composure slowly dissolve as she sat in one of my old leather client's chairs, chain-smoking endlessly and tearing at her fine hair until it hung like straw around her face.

I knelt in front of her chair and took her hands and held them until she looked at me. I looked back and saw the guilt she was drowning in, guilt from the death of two men I'd said I thought were not involved.

"Stop it," I said.

She looked at me with bleak resignation. "I did this," she whispered. "I caused this. If I hadn't hired you, if I hadn't pried into this, they would still be alive."

"You don't know that," I replied. "You can't. The truth might have come out. The killer might have killed them all anyway."

"It doesn't matter."

"It does. You're killing yourself with this. I won't let you do that, because I love you."

I held her as she lowered her head and wept. When I stood up again, I saw Bernstein looking hard at me.

"You are way over the line on this, man," he said. "You're going to hurt her bad."

"Fuck it," I snapped back. "We're all over the line on this one. The question is how we get out of it in one piece. I don't know how we do that."

"I do," Kate said, looking up. "We stop what we're doing before anyone else gets hurt. I mean that. We have to stop."

Bernstein dragged a chair over to Kate and sat down. "We can't do that, Kate," he said slowly. "Maybe we could, until yesterday. But now we know that Raines is still in the area, still working. We've talked to everybody who's connected with this case. They know we're here. Raines will, too. He may try to kill you before he's done. The only thing we can do is to keep going and drag this thing out of its hole and into the light. Otherwise we'll never know if you're safe."

We were about to try to work again when Marty Barnes,

the secretary who worked for me and two other lawyers, opened the door.

"Sorry, Matt," she began, "but there's a woman out here who insists on seeing you."

"What's her name?"

"She won't say."

Bernstein raised an eyebrow. I looked at him and shrugged. "Send her in," I said to Marty. We waited.

It was Diane Olmstead.

Her calm, arrogant facade had shattered like glass, the broken pieces of it scattered around her. She stood in my office door shaking from nerves and exhaustion, her eyes almost crazy with fear.

"Riordan, please. You've got to help me," she begged in a low, desperate voice. "They killed Stafa annd Kyle. And now they'll kill me. Her voice rose to a wail. "Oh, God, please. Please— "

"Stop it," I said harshly. "Calm down." I took her arm and walked her across my office. She walked jerkily, like a broken marionette, and sat heavily, still shaking.

I poured her three fingers of brandy from the office bottle. She picked up the glass and nearly dropped it. Brandy slopped on my desk.

"Use both hands," I said. She put both hands around the glass and forced it to her mouth. She got the brandy down in one long swallow and set the glass down. She fumbled in her purse and found a cigarette. She got it lit on her third try and swallowed the smoke hungrily.

"You're breaking training," I sneered. "That's gonna play hell with your time in the next 10K race. Where's your boy toy, lady? Young Christopher. Have him take care of you. I've got better things to do."

She lowered her head until her forehead touched the deck and sobbed. "Please," she said.

Kate said, "For God's sake, Matt, we've got to help her."

"No, we don't," I snapped. "She didn't care enough to help you by telling me what she knows. Goddammit, she lied to me." I walked over to Diane Olmstead and grabbed her hair. I picked her head up off the table, jerked it around so that she was looking at me. "Get this right, Diane. I don't care whether you live or die. You want some help, this time you buy it. With the truth." I let her go and walked away.

Kate poured her another shot of brandy and helped her drink it, the way you would help a child. I waited. The office was quiet. Time gathered like dust. Finally Diane Olmstead said "All right."

"You'll tell me what you know?"

"Yes. It's not very much."

"Don't kid yourself. It's enough to get you killed." I poured myself a drink and drank half of it and said, "You said they were going to kill you. Who were you talking about?"

"I just meant the people who killed Stephen and Kyle and Stafa. It must be someone who knows about Joshua."

"Who is Joshua?"

"It's not a person. It was a plan. Actually the name we gave to a plan."

"A plan for what? Did it have something to do with the power station bombings you were accused of?"

"I guess so." Her voice broke. "We did those bombings, you know. George got the dynamite. Some people hiding up in the mountains made the bombs. Steve and

Danny planted them. They didn't mean for that lineman to be hurt. They just wanted to blow up the power stations, shut off the power. You know, just destroy the property.''

"What did you do?"

"I drove."

"What about the others? Who else knew?"

"Deborah planned it. She researched which of the power substations should be hit to shut down power in Seattle. Kyle and Stafa knew about it. They helped set it up but didn't want to get involved in the actual bombings. So they kind of backed out."

"Who actually made the bombs?"

"I don't know. George had help, but I never found out from whom."

"Why did you blow up the substations?"

"They were practice, sort of. And to establish our credibility, for Joshua."

"What was Joshua? What was the plan?"

"I don't know it all. It was going to be a big bombing, some kind of really important target. We were going to plant the bombs and then detonate them if our demands weren't met."

"What were you asking for?"

"Money. For the Weather Underground and the Black Freedom Fighters."

"What was the target you were going to hit?"

"I don't know. We just called the whole thing Joshua."

"Do you know where it was?"

"No. Someplace in the northwest."

"Did you get outside help besides the people who made the bombs?"

"Some, I think. Elizabeth Doheny was here, and so was

Paul Reid, from the Weather Bureau, the Weather Underground head office. I'm pretty sure they were giving the orders.''

"Do you know who was going to plant the bombs?"

"No. I tried to stay away from it, because I was scared. But I was with George a lot, so it was hard not to hear some of it.''

"Did you actually go through with the plan?"

"It was started. Something went wrong, terribly wrong, I think. I never heard about it again. But when we were arrested for the substation bombing in Fall City, George said it was really important that we not tell anyone about Joshua, not even our lawyers.''

"What do you think happened?"

"I really don't know. Really.'' She hesitated and lit another cigarette.

"What was the target? What were you going to hit?"

"I don't know.''

"You're holding back.''

"No, honestly I'm not. Why don't you believe me?'' she cried.

"Forget it.'' I stood up and walked over to the door and opened it. "Take a walk, Diane. You don't get any help from me unless I get everything from you. See how far you get.''

"No. Please. Wait.'' She reached into her purse and took out a plain envelope. "I think that they tried to plant some bombs and one of them blew up. Like in that house in New York city in 1971. And that somebody got hurt, maybe killed.'' She handed me the envelope. "This is all the evidence I have.'' It's a page of notes that George took. They're in his handwriting.''

I tore open the envelope and took out a single sheet of notebook paper, the ordinary cheap punched kind they sell in college bookstores. It had been folded three times and the creases were dirty and brittle with age. The writing on the page was big and loosely scrawled. There was a rough sketch of two pipes joining together in a "Y." The writing read:

PLANT PRIMARY CHARGE AT JUNCTION OF FEEDERS TO INTAKE. 3K? SECOND CHARGE AT AUX. THIRD CHARGE AT MAIN DESK, ½K IN HOUSING. 30 MIN. ENOUGH? HOW FUSED?

I sat back in my chair and blew a stream of air at nobody in particular, stunned and strangely exhilarated. The truth was beginning to come out.

I turned to Diane Olmstead. "Why did you take this?" I asked.

She shut her eyes. "We had just been arrested for the Fall City bombings," she replied. "We'd been released on bail, and when I went home, George was waiting for me. He looked awful. He was pacing around the house and slamming the walls with his hands. He said everything had gone wrong, that she'd been hurt, and that none of us could tell anyone about Joshua. I didn't know what he meant, but it scared me. My lawyer had said it was lucky that no one had been killed at Fall City, because even if we hadn't actually planted the bombs, we could have been charged for murder if somebody died. I was afraid that was what'd happened."

"I think I understand," I said. "Felony murder. If anyone is killed in the course of committing a felony, even a coconspirator, you can be charged with first-degree murder. They've abolished it in some states, but it's still the law here."

"That's pretty much what my lawyer said. And I wanted something to protect myself. So I took a page of George's notes. He burned the rest."

"Who was the woman who was hurt?"

"I don't know. I never heard anything about it again. We were acquitted later, and we all just went on with our lives." She slumped in the chair, the adrenaline all burned out.

Silence hung in the air. I opened a window and clear cold air streamed in. After a while, I turned to Kate and said, "Call your bank. Have them send five thousand dollars here, in cash. Don't tell them why. If they ask any questions, threaten to buy the damned bank."

Kate picked up the telephone and spoke into it in low tones. She put down the receiver and said, "They'll be here in ten minutes."

"Good. Diane, there's a Mexicana flight at twelve-thirty that goes to Mexico City. From there you can go anywhere. Have you got a passport?"

"Yes."

"You were ready to run," I said grimly. "Bernstein will put you on the plane. Don't go home. Buy clothes when you get there. Don't use your credit cards. They can be traced. Go someplace where there are a lot of people, especially Americans. Maybe Bermuda. Or stay in Mexico."

"All right."

The money came a few minutes later. Bernstein took Diane Olmstead to the airport. Kate walked over to my desk and smoothed out the scrap of notebook paper. She stared at it for a long time. Then she closed her eyes.

I came up behind her and put my arms around her and held her.

"Is it bad?" she asked.

"It's bad enough. This isn't just like a demonstration or a protest. Protests are legal, and they're usually for good reasons. This is a long way from that. People got hurt, maybe killed. Do you really want to know?"

She was silent for a long time. Then she said, "No. But I want to finish this."

CHAPTER 19

Kate and I spent the rest of the day at the Public Library, hunched over the dim green glow of microfilm viewers, flipping through the slides of the Seattle and Portland newspapers for all of 1971 and most of 1972. I saw a half-dozen stories about bombings in the Northwest, including a series of attacks on the Bonneville Power Administration's transmission lines, blown up as a part of an extortion plan. None of them seemed to fit Diane Olmstead's story. The Bonneville attacks didn't involve a single, big target; they were scattered, hit-and-run assaults on isolated power towers. There were no reports of anyone being accidentally hurt or killed.

I shut off the viewer and rubbed the bridge of my nose. With my eyes closed the filmed pages still flipped by. I stood up and stepped behind Kate, still seated at the next viewer. I massaged her neck and shoulders with both hands. She shut off her machine and slumped in her chair, groaning under my touch.

"Lower," she said. "More with the thumbs."

"How are you feeling?"

"Better. I mean, I've got a headache and I'm nauseated from staring at this damned machine, but I feel better. Work is a great anesthetic, isn't it?"

"The next best thing to whiskey," I agreed. "Find anything?"

"Not much. When I saw the stories about the Portland post office being bombed at Christmas 1971, I thought that was it. But the timing is wrong. The Portland bombings happened after Steve's trial, and no one was hurt. Did you find anything?"

"No. This whole thing doesn't make sense," I sighed. "If Diane Olmstead was telling the truth, and somebody did get hurt or killed, there should have been all kinds of press coverage. Unless it was covered up somehow. That doesn't make sense either."

"What now?"

"Same thing. We've got to figure out what the target was," I said stubbornly. "Even if the bombing itself was covered up, God knows why, there's got to be a record of it somewhere we can dig up. But that means we'll first have to guess what happened." I began gently stroking Kate's neck. "My offer of Mexico is still open, Kate. Anytime."

She opened her eyes and turned to look at me, smiling sadly. "Soon," she said. "Bernstein's right. We can't just walk away."

"You're right, I suppose. But I still need a drink."

We stopped at the reference desk to turn in our rolls of microfilm. I xeroxed the page of Shields' notes Diane Olmstead had turned over to me, and Kate checked out a series of local maps and reference books to read over dinner. Kate's need to pursue her brother's killer had rekindled itself since Diane Olmstead had broken. The fire in her eyes was again as strong as when we'd first talked. It worried me a little. Her mood had changed too fast and too far. The line between devotion and mania is sometimes a narrow one.

We picked up Bernstein back at my office and drove over to the Bronze Dragon, in Chinatown. The Dragon is a big, overblown touristy sort of place with red and black lacquer serpents and hanging bead curtains all over the place. The food they usually serve to round-eyes would gag a goat, but you can eat pretty well if you talk to the owner and let him order for you. Especially if your idea of well is noodles in sesame paste with so much garlic that your kidneys start to hyperventilate.

It was early, and we found a big corner booth that gave Bernstein a line of sight to both entrances to the restaurant.

"Reasonable precautions," he told Kate.

She was amused. "So this way you can see them when they shoot you?" she asked.

"Well, that's the reasonable part," he replied.

When we finished eating, Kate pushed aside a platter of orange beef and spread a map of Washington State out on the table. "We didn't find out what happened," she said to Bernstein. "If bombs were actually planted and exploded, there should have been something in the papers, and there wasn't. Did Diane Olmstead say anything else on the way to the airport?"

"No. I think she told us all she knew."

"Damn. What we have to do is try to find the target," she said. "There's one other possibility, you know. They might have accidentally set off a bomb while manufacturing them. That might not show up in the city papers if they were out in the Cascades or eastern Washington. Well, let's start looking, anyway.''

We ordered another round of Chinese beer and started studying. I took the maps and learned that there were towns in Washington, Idaho, and Oregon named Jerome and Jefferson, John Day and Jackson, but none named Joshua. We looked at lists of banks and high schools and community colleges and hospitals, finding nothing. After three hours and a half-dozen beers I was ready to give up. Then I looked up and saw Kate's eyes widen.

"Oh, God," she said hollowly. "Oh, my God."

"What is it?"

She handed me a 1972 copy of the *Washington State Guide to Commerce and Industry*. She held it open, pointing to a half-page photograph.

The picture showed a white concrete dome rising out of the scrubby eastern Washington desert. Around the dome was a cluster of low buildings and two banks of short, wide steam stacks. A series of high-voltage transmission towers marched like giant stickmen into the desert.

The caption read:

CONTINENTAL NUCLEAR SERVICES OF KENNEWICK, WASH-INGTON, OPERATES THE JOSHUA M. STERN NUCLEAR PROJ-ECT, LOCATED ON THE HANFORD NUCLEAR RESERVATION. THE PLANT, WHICH NOW PRODUCES ELECTRICITY, IS JOINTLY OWNED BY THE U.S. ATOMIC ENERGY COMMISS-ION AND THE EASTERN WASHINGTON POWER SYSTEM.

"Joshua," she said.

I stared at the photo, reading the caption over and over again. Then I took the Xeroxed copy of George Shields's handwritten notes out of my pocket and read the words again, aloud: "PRIMARY CHARGE AT JUNCTION OF FEEDERS TO INTAKE. SECOND CHARGE AT AUX." I said, to nobody in particular, "Feeders. Water feeder lines? Intake. Intake for cooling water? Aux. Auxiliary Cooling system? Cut off the cooling water to a nuclear reactor and the heat builds up until the fuel melts. Three Mile Island. The China Syndrome. Neat."

There was a long silence around the table. Then Kate said, "It fits. It was big, and they could have extorted a lot of money for not exploding the bombs or a lot of publicity if they did. But suppose something went wrong. Maybe the bombs went off too soon and didn't do any real damage. The government could have covered that up." Then she added, slowly, "And that's what Steve meant when he said he could stop them from building more nuclear plants. Suppose he confessed, with some proof, to a partly successful terrorist attack on a nuclear power plant. It would be like Three Mile Island all over again. The federal government might even shut the existing plants down."

"It fits, all right," I said, "but how the hell do we prove it?"

"It's possible," Bernstein said. "It would be a hell of a job. No matter how hard they tried, they couldn't clean up all the files. Xerox copies would get lost. And think of all the records that would be involved—power generation and sales records, construction invoices, government appropriations. But it would take most of Kate's money to do it." He swallowed the rest of his beer and added, "There's an easier way. If you're sure that you're right, hit Shields with it. He's in politics, so he's exposed. He'll either fold or call your bluff. If he calls, go public. If we're wrong, the little bastard will sue—libel's the last refuge of dirty politicians and crooked businessmen these days—but so what? That's not the worst that can happen.''

I said to Kate, "If we're wrong, Shields will sue you and me for libel. It could be expensive."

She hardly thought about it at all. "Let's do it," she said, smiling. "It's only money. He'd be a shitty congressman anyway."

On the way home I stopped by my office to pick up the files for a couple of cases that were scheduled for hearing the next day. The night was quiet, and Occidental Street was empty. I told Bernstein to wait, I wouldn't be long.

There is nothing emptier than an office building at night. I walked up the three flights of stairs to my office. The building was dark. Pale-blue starlight drifted down from the skylights above the stairwells. Thin strips of yellow light leaked from cracks around the door of the escort service on the second floor. A muffled telephone rang in the escort agency office, a lonely empty sound on a slow Tuesday night.

If he had been there thirty seconds sooner he could have shot me with no trouble at all. I had just turned the key in my office door when I heard the doorknob of the fire door around the corner rattle. The door's pneumatic closer sighed as the door was pulled open. A footstep scraped on a rubber stair tread.

I flattened myself against the inside wall of my office and waited. The fire door was far enough around the corner that no one could get a straight shot into my office.

I pulled the .357 from my shoulder holster and pointed the gun straight up, ready to chop down on anyone walking around that corner.

The fire door clicked closed, softly. A step sounded on the wooden floor of the hallway. I took a quick look around the edge of the old-fashioned wooden doorframe. I saw the thick snout of a silenced machine pistol edging around the hallway corner.

I said, "Hello, Raines."

The machine pistol coughed softly and a couple of slugs chewed at the far side of my doorway.

I said, "You missed, Raines."

Down the hallway a deep voice chuckled. "Apparently so, Mr. Riordan," Raines said. He had a deep voice, and his English had the clip of the upper class, but with the long vowels of Afrikaans. "You know who I am, then?"

"I know who you are, Raines." I replied. "More to the point, I know what you are."

"That's rather better than I expected of you, Mr. Riordan. You might be marginally competent. You might even be armed."

"You're guessing, Raines. Care to find out?"

"I have never liked to guess, Riordan. I think we'll just have to wait." A match flared in the darkness, and I smelled cigarette smoke. "Care for a smoke, Riordan?" Raines asked. He tossed the pack into the hallway, just out of reach. Cellophane rattled as it hit the floor.

"Thanks, but I'm not dying for one."

He laughed again. "Puns *are* the lowest form of humor."

"Who hired you, Raines?" I asked. "What makes this whole thing so damned important that it's worth bringing you into it? You must be expensive."

"I am, Riordan. But I'm afraid I can't talk about those things. Not even to a dead man."

I said, "You're guessing again," but my voice sounded weak. My heart was beating high in my chest, and I was breathing in quick, shallow gasps. I thought hard. If I tried going back into my office, Raines would shoot me before I could even touch the windows. From where I stood I could not get off a direct shot. The only chance was to bounce straight across the corridor, turn, and shoot at the end of the hall, where Raines would come out of the stairwell. I would get just one clear shot, but I would have to kill him. If I failed, Bernstein and Kate would hear the shots. When they came into the building, they would be as pinned down as I was.

That was no good. I felt a sudden calm, like being in the lee of a storm at sea. I probably would not make it. But I thought I could make Raines pay the ferryman's fee.

I never got the chance.

There were footsteps on the stairs at the far end of the hall. Kate laughed and called out, "Hey, Riordan, we've got to get going, we've got crooks to catch."

Bernstein, suddenly sober, hissed, "Kate, get back. Something's—"

And the night exploded.

Raines came around the corner firing, his machine pistol stuttering softly, flaming in the dark. I stepped out from the doorway and shot him in the chest three times, the .357 roaring and kicking in my hands. The shots blew him back against the wall. He slid to the floor.

I ran down the hallway. Kate lay near the stairs, twisted on her side. The front of her sweater was soaked with blood. She was alive, but not by much. She choked and labored for breath. I fell on my hands and knees beside her, slamming the floor with my arms and fists as the world turned a dull aching red around me.

Bernstein shoved me roughly aside. "On your feet, goddammit," he roared. "Call the aid car. Move!"

Somehow I stumbled back to my office to call County Emergency, then ran back down the hall with the office first aid kit. I prayed to no one as I ran, not so much prayer as begging, that Kate would not die, that I would not hear her last rush of air before she made the silent flight alone.

Bernstein packed the entrance wound with gauze from the first aid kit and probed gently for an exit wound. He didn't find one. "Must have been a ricochet," he said. "Tumbling when it hit, but it hit slow. She has a chance, kid. But God only knows what it did inside."

Somehow Kate kept going, pulse thin, breathing slow, for the five minutes it took for the emergency team to get there. The medics took her away on a gurney and made Bernstein get off his feet while they packed the flat, shallow wound in his back. He must have gotten it while he was covering Kate. Neither of us had noticed it.

The first cops to get there wouldn't let me go to the hospital until Homicide arrived. I walked over by Raine's body and found his cigarettes on the floor. I smoked the cigarette he had offered me. I was empty of brains and thought and mostly of hope. He had been quite right. He was talking to a dead man.

They brought Kate out of surgery a little after midnight, with about equal chances of living or dying. They wouldn't let me see her or Bernstein, who had finally passed out from shock and blood loss after taking a bullet in the back that had cracked his shoulder blade. There would be nothing to do, they said, but wait.

Around one in the morning I found a pay phone and put a call through to the number Bernstein had for Arthur Case. The phone rang a long time. Case finally answered, sleepily.

"Who the hell is this?" he said, his thin voice petulant.

"It's Riordan, you bastard," I hissed. "You should know that Raines didn't solve your problem for you. He's dead. But Bernstein is still alive, and so am I, man. Our only question is whether we kill you ourselves or spread your little secrets across the newspapers so you can do it yourself."

"What are you talking about?"

"Bernstein was right, you fool. Raines was here, in Seattle. He came after me. I killed him. But not before he shot Katherine Warden. She probably won't live. My lover, Case. And for that I'm going to kill you."

"Wait a minute, Riordan, wait. Be sensible about this," he said calmly. "We can cut a deal. If there's something you want, I can get it for you."

"More than you dead? That's a hard one." I thought for a minute, listening to the hollow electronic noise on the line. I heard two soft clicks. Case was taping me, setting me up for something. I decided it didn't really matter.

"All right," I said. "Here's the deal. Not negotiable. A federally owned nuclear power plant, the Joshua Stern reactor at Hanford, Washington, was bombed in the summer or fall of 1971 by some homegrown college kid terrorists, probably connected to the Weathermen and God knows who else. At least one person was hurt or killed. I don't know if the reactor itself was damaged. You guys or somebody like you covered it up to protect the government and the nuclear industry. I want all the files on the bombing. I want them in six hours. You have two hours to call me back at this number.'' I gave him the number of the waiting-room pay phone.

''What do I get out of this?''

''A reprieve.''

''Not good enough, Riordan. I want Bernstein's evidence. All of it.''

I didn't know what the hell Bernstein had, but if it was on paper that was no problem. What are Xerox machines for? ''Agreed,'' I lied. ''With one small reservation.''

''What's that?'' he asked cautiously.

''If the woman dies, so do you. Two hours.''

CHAPTER 20

I blew down the long eastern slope of the Cascade Mountains like a Chinook wind and kicked ass at a hundred miles an hour across the high Columbia Plateau. Turning off the interstate at Yakima, I burned down the two-lane blacktop of old Highway 24 east to the Columbia River. There was a light dust of snow on the desert ground, and the Rattlesnake Hills loomed up like gray ghosts by the last tired light of a dying quarter moon. It was past four in the morning, but I felt no need for sleep. I was a hype. I was hyped on coffee and cigarettes and four tabs of speed, hyped on the biggest drug of them all, a rage that burned like cold fire in my head and rolled like glory through my veins

The Hanford Nuclear Reservation is a thousand square miles of bunch grass and lava rock above the Columbia River, the federal government's nuclear energy research and weapons center, the place where they put the atoms into atom bombs. It doesn't seem to bother the people who work and live there. They're used to it. Getting ready for Armageddon is just so much business as usual.

According to Arthur Case, Kate had been right. The Joshua Stern nuclear plant had been bombed, and damaged, in August 1971. The records, Case said, were still at the plant.

I stopped at a guard shack beside a fifteen-foot-high perimeter fence at the border of the reservation. I got out, stretched, lit another cigarette, and waited. A guard came out of the shack and walked over to me, carrying a clipboard. He had a young, round doughy face that barely emerged from the hood of a green military parka.

"Mr. Riordan?" he asked.

"That's right."

"Please step away from the car. I'm going to have to search it." He rested a hand on the revolver at his hip.

"Wait a second, kid," I replied. "I've got a piece. It's in a shoulder holster, but it'll come out butt first, and easy." I reached inside my coat and pulled out the gun. It was Bernstein's, a Spanish-made .380 automatic that he thoroughly detested. Ahlberg had impounded our guns each time there had been a shooting. After two shootings we were starting to run out of guns.

I handed the gun to the guard and waited while he searched the car, shivering in the thin, high desert wind. When he was through, he checked off something on his clipboard, saying, "Drive down this road about four miles until you get to the "J" Plant. Don't stop, and don't go off the road. You'll be met at the plant gate by a guy named Malenkov. He's head of security. I gotta keep the piece, but you can get it when you come back."

He handed me the clipboard to sign a form and looked at me under the harsh quartz lights from the guard shack. He said, "I don't feel good about letting you through. You got something in your eyes, man. Whatever it is, I hope you work it out." He stepped aside and waved me through.

Over the next ridge the Joshua Stern plant rose from the floor of the desert like an industrial-grade nightmare. The hundred-fifty-foot reactor dome was lit up by bright security lights and red aircraft-warning flashers. A cluster of low concrete machinery buildings clustered around the dome. I knew it was an old plant, but I was surprised at how shabby it looked, with peeling paint on the buildings and the night shift's parked cars scattered throughout the area. I had been expecting something high tech. This beast looked like a steel-rolling mill in Akron, Ohio.

I found a place to park and walked to a second gate. A man was waiting for me. He had a wide Slavic face with high cheekbones and slanting Asian eyes. He looked like he could pull a plow if he had to. He eyed me calmly and said, "My name's Malenkov. You must be Riordan."

"I am," I agreed. He opened the fence, and I walked through it and into an office. He opened a desk and took out some visitor forms and a couple of radiation badges. He was starting to fill out one of the forms when I stopped him.

"You're probably not going to want a record of this," I said.

He tossed his pen down on the counter and said, "I control security here, Riordan. You'll do as I say. Now, what the hell is this all about?"

"You government guys are always talking about the need to know, Malenkov. Well, listen up. All you need to know is, you've got orders from the Secretary of Energy, maybe even the White House, to show me some old files. You didn't believe those orders, but you checked them out, and they were for real. If you don't follow them, you'll be walking perimeter fence on the reservation this winter. So get on with it."

He gave me a long stare that could have blistered paint. Then he handed me a radiation badge and turned and stalked out the door. I followed him.

He led me across the plant yard and down a long stairway to a records storage area underneath the turbine building, next to the reactor itself. Above us the coolant pumps forcing water into the reactor chugged and vibrated like the washing machine at the end of the universe. Acres of green file cabinets stood in columns that fanned out across the room. If Malenkov was as smart as he was tough, he'd just wave at the file cabinets and tell me to start looking.

We walked into an office tucked in the corner of the arena-sized records room. A tall woman with broad shoulders was standing at a counter leafing through a black loose-leaf book. She had a strong, serious, competent face that was filled, at the time, with sleepy confusion.

"Hello, Greg," she said to Malenkov. "I got the codes you sent down, but I can't find the files. It's a vault code, but I can't find them."

"Don't worry about it," Malenkov said. "Jane Brant, this is Riordan. He's the reason you're up this early." He turned back to me and said, "Ms. Brant is the chief records custodian."

She shook my hand, distracted. "I still don't get it, Greg. The files have to be here. The NRC requires that everything be kept on the manifest. I even plugged the codes into the computer, and it just gives me a null.''

"Don't worry about it, Jane. These codes aren't on your list. Come on, let's get to the vault.''

Brant led us through the maze of file cabinets to a vault room set in the center of the room. She slipped an identity card with a magnetic code strip into a slot in the wall and took a key from a chain around her neck. When the light above the slot flashed green, she inserted the key and turned it. A steel-reinforced bank door swung open on noiseless hinges.

Malenkov walked into the vault between banks of reinforced file cabinets. A second vault door was set into concrete in the rear of the vault. He started to open it.

"Jesus. No wonder.'' Jane said.

"What's in there?'' I asked.

"You don't want to know,'' she muttered. "Plutonium production records. Warhead designs.''

Malenkov opened the second door, then unlocked a file cabinet inside. He came out with a dusty cardboard file box and set it on a table in the main vault.

"Go ahead, Riordan,'' he said with surprising bitterness. "It's all there.''

I opened the box. It was full of files and envelopes. I took a report bound in red plastic from the front of the box. It was labeled ATOMIC ENERGY COMMISSION: SECRET. GRADE A6 EYES ONLY. I opened it. The title on the flyleaf was INQUIRY INTO THE BOMBING ATTACK AND SUBSEQUENT CORE MELT EVENT AT JOSHUA STERN NUCLEAR POWER STATION, 19 AUGUST 1971.

"Jesus Christ,'' I said. "You had a meltdown. The China Syndrome.''

"No, it wasn't," Malenkov replied. "We lost reactor coolant for about eighteen minutes. We had high temperatures, and some of the fuel rods fused. But four guys in radiation suits were able to operate the auxiliary cooling system manually to save the plant. There wasn't even much radioactive release. We had it cleaned up and back in service in six months."

"You were here, weren't you, Malenkov? You know what happened. Tell me."

He brushed a hand through his thick black hair and sighed. "They tried to plant three charges," he said slowly. "They planted two, one at the main cooling intake line, one in the pumps. We don't know when. Probably days before they tried to set the third, in the control room. That was the hard part, since it is always manned. They waited until the shift change, at midnight on the eighteenth. Somehow they got there when the crew was out of the room. They apparently got surprised when the crew chief for the third shift, a guy named Wells, came on. All three charges exploded."

"What happened to them?"

"What do you think?" he said angrily. "They were using gelignite. There wasn't enough left to identify anybody. There wasn't anything at all." He reached over and turned the pages of the report to the back. "Here are the employee applications for the people who did the bombing. They gave their names as Bill Greer and Naomi Martin. Both phony, of course." He turned the page. "Their college transcripts were from the Engineering College at Oregon State. Greer was hired as a coolant chemistry technician. Martin worked as a gofer in plant operations.

We had their fingerprints on their applications but turned up nothing. Neither of them had a record.''

"Did you connect them to anybody else?"

"Never. They were good, I tell you. Maybe Soviet-trained."

I laughed. The pain and anger and worn-down nerves let go and I laughed. Malenkov glared at me. "You're wrong, man," I said. "So wrong. They were amateurs. College kids."

I opened an envelope. There were photographs inside. The top photo on the stack showed a damaged control room. The trunk of a charred corpse lay beside a damage control panel. I dropped the stack of photographs on the table and gagged, nearly falling.

"My God," I said. "I'm sorry."

"We think that was Wells," he said tightly. "We think."

"How could you let them get that far?" I asked.

"Oh, hell, I don't know," he said angrily. "I was a kid at the gates, just out of the army, and security was as good a job as I could get. In those days we never thought that something like this could happen, that Americans could kill one another, destroy government property, risk thousands of lives, just because they weren't happy about the way things were going in the country. Security wasn't built around stopping terrorists willing to take chances or work from the inside. Back then you could get a job in a nuclear plant with two years of college engineering for the tough jobs, just high school for a technician. We ran all the normal security checks. They passed. Goddammit, they passed." Malenkov clapped one of his big fists in the other and wrung it out. "It will never happen again."

"Maybe not," I replied, "but this one isn't over yet."

"What do you mean, Mr. Riordan?" Jane Brant asked. She had been quiet through Malenkov's long harangue, stunned at what she'd learned. She was fingering the photographs and crying, softly.

"It means I have to take these," I answered, gesturing at the documents. "For a while, anyway."

Malenkov grabbed my arm. "No."

I grabbed him by the front of his coat and slammed him up against the wall of the cabinets. His head cracked against the metal. He got a big arm loose, and he clubbed me on the side of the head with a fist like a block of iron. It staggered me back but I cuaght him as he came up after me.

"Listen to me, you fool," I hissed. "Listen. I've come at this thing from the other side. Some of the people who planned this are still alive. And somehow the news of this bombing didn't stay buried. There have been five murders in the past four weeks connected to these bombings, Malenkov. Maybe six." I closed my eyes and pushed thoughts of Kate out of my mind. "Whoever killed those people was afraid of this coming out. I can get the killer for you, Malenkov. I know who it is. I can put him away. But I have to have the evidence."

He shook his head. "This country needs nuclear power, Riordan. If you let this out, it will kill the industry. The plants will be shut down. Thousands of people will lose their jobs. You don't have the right to do that."

"Maybe not." I said. "But the people who live with nuclear plants have the right to know what the risks are, and the right to decide if they want to take them. You can't bury the truth forever. When you do, it festers. And kills. Read the papers, man. Nine people have already died over this. Your three. My six. Isn't that enough?''

Malenkov thought it over silently. Then he said, ''My orders don't cover this. What it boils down to is, I have to trust you. All right, take this stuff. We'll cover it as long as we can. Jane, are you with me on this?''

''Yes,'' she said simply.

Malenkov took the report and the pictures, straightened them into a pile, and handed them to me. He picked up the box. ''Come on,'' he said. ''I'll get you off the reservation.''

We drove off the Hanford Reservation through the south gate and through the just-waking suburban town of Richland on our way to the airport in Pasco. Malenkov waited as I turned in Bernstein's rental car and called Ahlberg and told him to meet me in Seattle. He waited as I broke a credit card line down to nothing chartering the only plane available, a Lear. He walked me out to the plane.

''Do the right thing,'' he said.

''I'm going to get the killer,'' I replied. ''That's the only thing I can do. After that, things will have to take care of themselves.''

''Good enough,'' he said.

CHAPTER 21

I read the Atomic Energy Commission's report about the bombings on the plane back to Seattle. The report confirmed most of what Malenkov said. The attack on the plant had been almost absurdly easy. The terrorists—I found it hard to think of anybody who'd gone to Oregon State as a terrorist—had been hired on the strength of false college transcripts four months before the bombings. No one had checked the transcripts.

Once hired as low-level technicians, they had relatively free access to the engineering drawings of the plant. They could also go to any part of the plant except the fuel-handling areas. The first two bombs had been planted in the primary and secondary cooling systems, which had been badly damaged. The third charge had exploded inside the control room itself.

The report concluded that both Greer and Martin had been killed in the blast, even though bodies could not be identified, or even pieced together, after the explosion and fire that swept through the control room. The federal security people got almost no evidence from the control room, because the room could not be sealed until after the reactor was back under control. It probably didn't seem important at the time. The reactor had come within a few minutes of a nuclear meltdown, when the heat of the fissioning uranium would crack the containment dome and send a cloud of steam, laden with deadly plutonium, into the clear desert sky. The reactor staff hadn't cared about the evidence. They'd wanted to save their own lives.

It really didn't matter. Within a few hours, the Atomic Energy Commission had decided to cover the whole thing up.

I sighed and set the report aside, sipping at my coffee and trying to think. Maybe it was the hours or the speed or the grief that left me with an empty burning in my chest, but knowing the truth about the Joshua bombing didn't tell me who had killed Stephen Turner. In a way it made the problem worse: one more jarring misfit piece of a puzzle that already looked like some kind of surrealist collage. Even when I took them one at a time, the pieces made no sense.

The FBI had never found the Pacific Liberation Front, but that didn't mean they weren't real. Diane Olmstead had said that the Joshua plant bombing had been planned by the Weathermen, the national leaders in the radical movement. Some of them were still around; Paul Reid, the Columbia professor who'd taken up radical politics and robbing banks, had been underground for years. The old Radical Left might not want an unfinished piece of business coming to the surface, focusing attention on them, at a time when they had other plans, other lives to protect.

The drug connections at the edge of the case were real and were probably what had given Henry Cruz reason for wanting me to stay the hell away from Danny Schoen. That didn't explain why somebody had planted coke in Turner's apartment, the other deaths, or why Danny Schoen's own backup man had wasted him in the street. No way.

Now that I knew the Joshua bombing had been covered up, the government itself looked like a suspect. If Stephen Turner had planned to go public with the information on the bombings, a lot of now-very-senior officials implicated in the cover-up would be looking at their own ruin in the mirror every morning, wondering whether today would be the day. That would give them strong reason to eliminate every witness. But the government hadn't been able to find the witnesses before, and Case had been almost too willing to trade me the evidence on the bombing for his own sweet neck. If somebody serious had their ass on the line, he would never have made the trade. And the killings had been too nasty, too public, not in the bureaucratic style that leaned to youthful heart attacks and one-car accidents on rain-slick roads.

So, scratch the government.

It still didn't make any sense.

Drugs and terrorists and a government cover-up and five people dead in the streets.

I had just one thing left. I had a live witness I could tie to the Joshua bombings with enough proof to make him sweat. A witness with very good reasons of his own for wanting all his old friends dead.

George Shields.

The chartered plane dropped out of the clouds and, caught by a wind shear, bounced twice on the tarmac at Boeing Field. When I got off the plane, Vince Ahlberg was waiting for me, standing beside a dark-blue Chrysler sedan with a silent blue emergency light clipped to its roof, flashing in the gray morning light.

"Jesus," he said as I got off the plane. "You look like shit. Where the hell have you been?"

"I'll explain on the way. Have you found Shields?"

"He's waiting for us at his home. He's not going anywhere. I've got two county uniforms parked outside his door. He and his old man are not happy. This had better be good."

We got into the car and pulled away into the morning traffic on Interstate 5. "It goes back fifteen years," I began. "Shields and Turner and the others began to work with the Weathermen, planning bombings in the Northwest. They really did do the bombing of that power station at Fall City they were tried for in 1971. And at least one other. They tried to bomb the Joshua Stern nuclear reactor out at the Hanford Reservation. They didn't completely wreck the reactor, but three people died in the blast."

Ahlberg shook his head, eyes still staring ahead at the road. "You able to prove any of this?"

"Some. Not much. The bombing at the nuclear plant did happen. The Atomic Energy Commission covered it up, but I've got their reports and some of the other documents from their investigation. I've got some of Shields's handwritten notes that seem to be talking about the reactor. And Diane Olmstead can tie him in to the Weathermen."

"That's enough to wreck his campaign, but you still

can't prove he did the bombings. Or that he's connected to these killings.''

''Maybe not. But he's got one hell of a motive for wanting to kill the others.''

''Maybe. Let's see what he's got to say.''

We rode in silence through the gray morning. Ahlberg drove across the floating bridge over Lake Washington and snaked his way through the quiet green suburban streets along the shore.

George Shields lived in a gray shingled house overlooking the water, amid a tangled lush growth of cedar and alder tees. When we got there, he was waiting for us in a high-ceilinged study, already dressed in a dark-blue politician's suit, staring moodily out at the dark-gray waters of the lake.

''I've already canceled two appearances this morning, Lieutenant,'' he said stiffly. ''I hope that this is important, not merely some nonsense that Mr. Riordan there has dreamed up to harass and intimidate me.''

''That's an interesting choice of words, George,'' I said nastily, ''considering that five people you knew well have been killed in the last four weeks. 'Harass' and 'intimidate' are the kind of words I use when I think my client's guilty.''

''Matthew, shut up,'' Alhberg snapped. To Shields, he said, ''Let's understand one another. This is an informal interview, Senator. You are not under arrest. I am not yet accusing you of anything.''

''All right,'' Shields said curtly. ''What do you want?''

''Just to talk,'' Ahlberg replied. ''About the deaths of Stephen Turner, Deborah Greene, Daniel Schoen, Kyle Parman, and Mustafa Kemal. In fact, Senator, almost everybody connected with the Northwest Nine trial is dead. Except you. Why is that?''

"How should I know?'' he replied irritably. Shields poured himself coffee from a silver pot set on a low server. "Everything I've read points to a group of crazy terrorists. That doesn't make me a suspect.''

"No,'' Ahlberg agreed. "But it may make you a victim.'' He walked across the room and poured himself a cup of coffee. "I'm too old a cop to believe in coincidences. These killings are tied together. We're beginning to think that the motive for these murders is connected to the bombing at Fall City. And,'' he added casually, "the bombing at the Joshua Stern Nuclear Power Plant at Hanford.''

He looked at Shields and waited patiently.

Shields handled it pretty well. He walked to his desk and took a cigar from a humidor and clipped the end, staring at it. Then he tossed it on the desk with a snort. "You've really gone off the deep end, Lieutenant. You must be desperate. I assume this is something Riordan cooked up. As for this reactor or whatever, I don't know what you're talking about.''

"Yes, you do, George,'' I told him. "Early in 1971 you met with some of the head people from the Weathermen. Paul Reid. Elizabeth Doheny. You sat down with them and Turner, Greene, and Schoen. You planned the Fall City bombing as a kind of a dry run, I think. You recruited a couple of people, a man and a woman, who called themselves Greer and Martin. They went to work at the Joshua Stern nuclear plant in April of 1971. In August that year they planted explosives. Three charges. The first two at the main and auxiliary cooling water intakes. The third was supposed to go in the control room. Only it didn't work. They got caught planting the third charge. It went off. They died, along with a reactor operator named Wells. There wasn't much left of the bodies, Shields. Almost nothing. Here. Take a look." I stood up and tossed the black-and-white photos of the charred partial corpse on his desk.

Shields stood casually behind his desk, ignoring the photographs on the desktop. He started to say "You've got no right—" when something snapped in my head and I grabbed him by the scruff of his fat neck, forcing his head down to the desktop.

"Look at them, you little bastard," I hissed. "Look at what you've done. See the charred body? Like napalm, man, like napalm."

I tossed him aside and stepped away, disgusted. Shields had stumbled a little as he looked at the pictures, and now he leaned on the desktop for support. But he shook his head doggedly, like a fighter trying to get clear.

"No way," he said hollowly. "No way. You can't prove anything."

"I can prove a little," I replied. "After the bombing at the nuclear plant went wrong, you panicked. You told Diane Olmstead about meeting with Liz Dohey and Paul Reid and warned her never to talk about it. She can testify to that, and she will. When I pressed you about the name Joshua, you panicked again. You went running down to Danny Schoen. I followed you down there, saw your car at his club before his goons grabbed me and busted me up. What were you doing there, Shields? Saving Danny's soul? That would take a hell of a lot of work."

He had decided to fight it out. He worked a sneer onto

his face and said, "That it? If it is, you can stop wasting my time now."

"Not quite," I replied. I took out the Xeroxed copy of Shields's notes on the plan for the bombings and laid it quietly on his desk.

He read it slowly, fear spreading across his face and breaking like a wave hitting the shore. "Where did you get this?" he whispered painfully, his palms flat on the desktop, his head bowed. "Where?"

"Diane took it from you, man. She didn't trust you worth a damn, and she took it in case she ever needed to save her own life. She gave it to me, and I got her out of town so your killer couldn't find her. You might as well talk to us. You're all out of choices."

"I didn't kill them," he said hoarsely.

"Sure, you did," Ahlberg said in a tough, quiet voice. Sometime during my speech he had made up his mind that Shields knew more than he'd admitted, and now he was going to try and break him. "You had Turner killed because he was going to confess to the bombing of the nuclear plant as a way to raise the issue of safety in public. You came up with the terrorism line as a cover. You also planted the drugs in Turner's apartment to make it look like he had drug connections. You probably never planned to kill the others. But when Riordan came around and started to dig into the Northwest Nine trial you panicked again. So you had them all killed."

"No," Shields said, choking out the words. "No. I couldn't kill anybody."

"You're forgetting," Ahlberg said coldly, "that you helped murder three people in 1971."

"I've got nothing to say." It was a broken whisper.

"That doesn't matter," Ahlberg said diffidently. "It may take us another day or a week or a month to find the evidence we need, but we'll get it. You're not going anywhere, Mr. Shields. When I come for you next time, it will be for real." Ahlberg smiled a small, cold half smile.

Shields began to cry. "Get out of here," he sobbed. "You have to leave. I want to talk to my lawyers. Leave."

"Talk all you want," I told him. "But you're through, man. Too many people are hurt or dead. This time you don't walk away. If I have to put you in a box myself."

Ahlberg fed him more of the same smile. "We're leaving," he said quietly. "Matthew, you're coming with me. Now. Don't blow my bust."

We left. As we drove away I rolled down the car window. The air was thick with moisture, like trying to breathe through damp cotton wool. I forced it into my lungs. It didn't help. I had been running on nerves for too long, and there was nothing left for me to do but go to the hospital and sleep and hope that I would hear Kate's voice when I woke.

I was silent on the ride back to town. Ahlberg finally said, "You got something bothering you? You seem dissatisfied."

"I was just thinking on the system of justice," I replied. "Thinking that if we had been dealing with anybody but a rich connected guy like Shields you might have taken him down to the cop shop and played psychological handball with his head for six or seven hours and then lost him in the county jail for a week or two to see if that helped his memory."

"That all?"

"Not quite. I was also thinking how much I wanted to kill him."

"I thought you might be a little hostile. Stay away from him, Matthew. Let me work this thing out my way. Shields isn't going anywhere. I've got people watching him, and I want to see what he does under some pressure." His voice softened a little and lost its warning tone. "You've done more than anyone could have asked. Now just stay the hell away from it, and let me do my job."

"Okay," I replied. "Anyway, how do you figure it now?"

"I think he killed them all," he replied.

CHAPTER 22

I think I heard the explosion in my sleep, a distant rumbling like summer thunder on the plains of Central Montana. At least that's the way I dreamed of it, the rumble and the flash of white light in the dark sky.

Then Bernstein was shaking me roughly awake. He was dressed in jeans and was zipping a windbreaker over his bare hairy hide, the only thing he could get on over the bandages on his back. "Let's go, kid," he said. "There's been a bombing. And the television people say that this Pacific Liberation Faction has called in to take credit again."

I splashed water from a hospital jug on my face and swallowed the rest of the cold coffee from a cup on the arm of my chair.

"Okay," I said groggily. "They say where the bombing was?"

"Downtown someplace. An office. In that godawful black bank building."

"Pacific National? Where Shields works?"

"Christ, I don't know. I guess so."

I ran out of the hospital, Bernstein chugging along behind, trailing officious nurses and bewildered orderlies in our wake.

As we got into the car Bernstein demanded, "What gives here? And what did you find out at Hanford, anyway? You were asleep by the time I found out you were here."

"They really did it, man. They bombed that nuclear plant, just as Kate guessed. Turner, Greene, Shields, and maybe some of the others planned it. They managed to put two people inside the plant. The inside people were surprised by one of the plant workers when they were planting the last charge. It went off. They were killed. The plant nearly had a meltdown. The goddamn government hushed it up."

"Any evidence?" he demanded.

"Ahlberg's got it. But they never found out who the inside people were. Ahlberg and I braced Shields about it this morning. He had them all killed, Bernstein. He has to be the one. Ahlberg didn't take him in, preferred to put a tail on him. But if that was his office . . . Christ, I don't know."

We squealed our way through the parking lot and took the side streets down the hills to the downtown financial district as fast as I dared.

The cops had closed off Third Avenue a block south of Seneca. I double-parked and ran to the barricade, looking up at the black-glass bank tower.

The explosion had torn a gaping hole in the south facade of the building, near the top. Broken glass had fallen like hail on the streets below. I shoved through a crowd of spectators to the police line. When I ducked under the crime-scene ribbon, two uniformed bulls grabbed me, but not before I spotted Wechsler, the wire-thin homicide detective.

"Hey, Wechsler!" I shouted. He turned around and walked over, his long, thin legs stiff as stilts.

"Who was it?" I demanded. "Was Shields—"

"Yeah," he said sourly. He rooted in a pack of cigarettes and pulled out a twisted limp smoke. "Yeah. It was Shields."

"What happened?"

"The bomb was in the desk. George sat down to do some work, opened a drawer. BAM. His office has a new color scheme."

"What about the Liberation Faction?"

"Same deal as last time," he said listlessly. "Guy gets killed, then a telephone call to Mark Sitwell at the *Post* with a little message. What the hell's going on with you, Riordan? Three hours ago Ahlberg calls me and says you've got the thing cracked, that Shields is hiring the killings done. Now Shields is dead." He took his cigarette out of his mouth, dropped it, and stamped on it angrily. "Who the fuck are these people, anyway? How do they just walk in and kill somebody and walk away? How?"

"Christ, I don't know. I don't know anything. It seems like I never did."

Wechsler put a hand on my shoulder and said, "I heard about Mrs. Warden, Matt. Is she gonna be all right?"

"They're not sure. She's hanging on, for now."

"I'm sorry."

"Yeah."

"You want to talk to Ahlberg?"

"I guess so. Where is he?"

"Up in the building. Come around front in ten minutes or so. I'll take you up."

I found Bernstein and told him what had happened. Then we walked around to the front of the bank building through one of those windswept concrete plazas that architects always put in front of skyscrapers. It was raining again, and the wind blew the rain in our faces as we walked through the plaza.

Wechsler was waiting for us. He took us up to see Ahlberg.

The cops had set up shop in the Shields firm's conference room. When we arrived, Ahlberg was swiveling back and forth in a big leather conference chair with a phone tucked under his ear. He waved us over. Then he swore and hung up the phone.

"No dice on the trace," he said. "But Sitwell tried; give him credit for that. The best the phone company can say is someplace east of the lake. The whole goddamn country is east of the lake." He sighed and looked at us. "So, what have you two masked marauders got to say, Riordan? This morning you had me convinced that Shields had to be the killer. Now what?"

"I don't know," I confessed. "We took it as far as we could. Don't say we didn't pay for it. We paid."

"Yeah. Your client did," he said sourly. "Why the hell didn't you just back off when we asked you. You could have sold her on it. At least she wouldn't have got shot. Anyway, stick around. Broderick wants to talk to you."

Ahlberg picked up the phone and punched numbers.

Harmon Broderick, the agent in charge of the Seattle FBI office, walked in a few minutes later.

"We've still got nothing on the Pacific Liberation Faction," he said to Ahlberg. "We've had people undercover in the peace-nut and antinuke groups for three weeks now. They haven't heard a thing. We're going to have to do it the hard way—interview all the people working in the building, check out all the sources of explosives in the area."

He poured himself a Styrofoam cup of coffee from a carafe on the table and slurped it noisily. He looked me over dispassionately.

"You're Riordan, right?" he said finally. "Listen, we've got to talk to the Olmstead woman. She's the last one of these old radicals still alive. She must know who this Pacific Liberation Group is."

"I don't think she does," I said. "She gave us a lead to the Joshua bombing, but that's all she knew. I don't know where she is. We put her on a plane."

"Cute," he said in a low, deadly voice. "Very cute. Helping a suspect leave the jurisdiction. You're looking at obstruction of justice charges, you jerk."

"Bullshit," I said angrily. "The Bureau's been obstructing justice for thirteen years in the Joshua Stern plant bombing. I didn't bugger that one, Broderick. You or somebody like you did. I dragged it out in the open."

"I want to see the documents on this fantastic story of yours, Riordan. I want them right now."

"I gave them to Ahlberg." I turned to Vince. "Don't give them to him. The Bureau will just bury them again. For God's sake, it's still the only lead we've got."

Ahlberg stared at Broderick. What he was looking for, I

don't know. "I'll call the office and tell them to start Xeroxing them, Harm," he said calmly. "You can have a copy in an hour or so."

Broderick returned Ahlberg's icy stare, then stormed out.

"Well, well," Ahlberg said mildly. "Never can tell when the Bureau's got its ass on the line, can you? By the way, Matthew, I dug out the old SPD intelligence unit files two days ago. There isn't much of anything there to help us. But there were a couple of good cops involved in the undercover work. Good cops working for a dumb mayor and a fascist S.O.B. of a chief. Will you trust me on this one, let me keep them out of it? I'm trusting you."

"Yes," I replied. "And thanks. But keep an eye on those files from the Joshua Stern plant bombing. You might get visited by the boys with the black bags later on tonight."

"No problem."

I poured myself some coffee and sat down. "How's Shields's father?" I asked.

"He's usually a son of a bitch," Ahlberg answered, "but not anymore. You want to talk to him?"

"Just for a minute."

"Okay." He turned to a uniformed cop and sent him out. The cop walked back in with George Shields's father a moment later.

"Yes, lieutenant?" he said quietly.

The death of a child before a parent is an unnatural thing. It had broken Shields. Enough time had passed for him to get past the shock, put on his public face again, a supreme act of control in the lifetime of maintaining control that most successful lawyers lead. But the effort had cost him, probably forever, the brick-hard self-assurance of a man in his prime. In two hours that morning he had crossed the border from middle to old age. He would never cross back again.

"Riordan here wants to talk to you."

"Will it take long? Mrs. Shields is returning from San Francisco in an hour. She doesn't know. I need to tell her myself."

"It won't take long, Mr. Shields. Two things. First, I was wrong about your son, at least partly wrong. I'm sorry for your loss."

"Yes," he said stiffly. "I believe you are."

"Second, do you own a house or a farm near Roslyn, Washington?"

"No. Not anymore. I did take a house there in lieu of a fee back in the early sixties. It wasn't worth much; Roslyn was pretty empty after the coal mine shut down. George used it for skiing and hiking, mostly. George finally sold it a few years back. I don't know who it was sold to."

"Where is it?"

"Just through town, last road on the right. Only house on the road, down at the end. Is this relevant?"

"I don't know. I guess not."

"I'm sorry. I have to leave now. The plane will be arriving." He turned and went.

Ahlberg said, "What's so important about this house?"

"The younger George probably used it as a crash pad for SDS people and other student radicals passing through," I told him. "I thought it might be worth a search. But if it's been sold, we can forget it."

"Keep me posted on what you're doing," Ahlberg said.

"I'm not going to do anything, Vince. I'm all through.

I've done everything I know how to do, and I've fucked up the rest. I'm just going to try and get Kate well enough to take her as far away as possible from this horror so she can forget that it ever happened.''

Bernstein stood up to go. His wound had stiffened up, and he held himself carefully. He and Ahlberg traded looks, and each nodded a fraction of an inch at the other, as though they expected to meet again. In a lineup.

Bernstein and I left with that at-loose-ends feeling that comes when something big in your life has finished, but not finished well. We drifted down to Pioneer Square with the thought of hitting ourselves over the head with a bourbon bottle, but our hearts weren't in it. The whiskey lacked warmth. It didn't cut the bitter, tired taste in my mouth or the weary ache in my bones of too many waking hours.

We walked back to my office. In the hallway plasterers were patching the bulletholes left by Raines's machine pistol.

I scrounged up some beer for us and settled down to paw listlessly through my mail. I played wastebasket basketball with most of it, then found an oversize envelope that had been delivered via courier. The return address said it was from the United States Department of Energy.

I opened it carefully. Inside I found two pieces of cardboard taped together, and a note. The note read:

Mr. Riordan—
After you left I traced back through the personnel records of the suspected bombers to see what might still be there. I found these photos and had them enlarged. I hope they help.
　　Jane Brant

I slit the tape carefully. The photographs were in black and white but with a little better quality than the usual ID picture. The first picture showed a young woman of twenty or so. She had a round face, long hair, and large light eyes, very wide and innocent, very beautiful. I couldn't shake the notion that I had seen her before.

About the next picture I had no doubt. The man was younger and lacked a beard, but the face was the same. The eyes had that naked look people who wear glasses have when they take them off for a picture.

I knew him, all right. It was Thomas Darwin.

CHAPTER 23

If you're going to do a bit of theater, you have to dress for it. I was. I wore black stretch jeans, black socks, black running shoes. I wore a black turtleneck sweater and a black watch cap. I even wore a black gun in a black holster. I hoped I was scary. At least I was color-coordinated.

Bernstein did not like it one damned bit. "This is stupid, Matthew. Really stupid. I agree that Darwin is probably the killer. Fine. Either send the cops after him, or, if you're really sure, let things ride for a week or two and I'll whack him out quietly. You're an amateur. Going after him yourself is crazy. You'll get your ass shot off or walk into a booby trap like George Shields did."

"Maybe."

"So, listen to me. Do what I say. Think of me as your violence consultant."

I laughed but stopped when I saw Bernstein's worried face. "Look," I said. "Neither of your ways works.

There's absolutely no evidence that ties him to Raines, to Cruz, or to any of the murders. None. They couldn't even get him for the bombings at the Stern plant. What evidence would they have? Well, he disappeared after the bombing. So what? He could say he tried to stop it, got hurt, and left in a daze. He could even feign amnesia. And you know what? He'd walk. Because everybody who could tie him to that bombing is dead.''

"That still leaves my second choice."

"I'm not God, Bernstein. Neither are you. We could be wrong. And I'm not willing to live with the thought that we killed him without knowing for sure."

"You don't even know he's up in the mountains."

"He's there. He isn't at his apartment and his office says he's out of town. I think he bought that house up in the mountains, in Roslyn. It's got some kind of meaning for him."

Bernstein sighed, exasperated. "Okay. What will you do if you find him?"

"Confront him with the facts." I slipped on a pair of thin black-leather gloves, wriggling my fingers until they were tight. "Reason with him. Persuade him."

"And if that doesn't work?"

"I don't know."

"I'm going with you.'

"No. If I mess up, I want you to pick up the pieces. Help Kate. And then you can use Plan B. You'll be sure."

Roslyn was an old coal-mining town, set in a cleft in a long ridge running east and north into the Cascade Range. When the coal pits played out, the town was reborn as a jumping-off point for hikers and skiers to the Alpine Lakes

Wilderness. A few artists and poets followed, looking for and mostly finding low rents, cheap beer, and good times.

In the car I swallowed two more tabs of speed and washed them down with lukewarm coffee. I hadn't gotten but two hours sleep in the last forty-eight, and I could feel the jolt from the speed almost right away. It felt good. If I kept it up, whatever I knew that passed for reality would dissolve into the drugs. But I had purpose. If I could hold on to that, it would be enough.

Roslyn was pretty much sleeping as I drove through. Most of the houses were dark, with only the blue television glow leaking out through half-drawn drapes. Even the tavern, glimpsed through double glass doors, was empty and quiet.

I cut my lights and drove under the starlight until I reached the last side road at the north end of town. I parked in the weeds behind a house with a sign in front that advertised handmade candles and pottery. From there I walked in the ditch beside the road.

It was a wide, low house, maybe seventy-years-old, with traces of carpenter Gothic in the sawed filigree trim around the porch. The lights in the front room were still switched on. The house was on the same side of the road that I was. I walked in a wide circle through the trashy third-growth woods to come up on it from behind.

When I was close enough, I snaked in on my belly around the side of the house to the front porch. I crawled up to the windows. Thomas Darwin sat in three-quarter profile, working at an old rolltop desk. He didn't know I was there.

No time like the present. I took Bernstein's lousy but

unregistered .380 automatic out of my shoulder holster, rolled to my feet, and kicked in the front door.

Darwin got a hand in the desk drawer about the same time that the .380 roared and my round crashed into the desk about two inches above his left shoulder. I crossed the room in two steps and stomped the drawer shut on his hand. The bones cracked, and he screamed. He curled himself into a fetal tuck around his damaged hand. I yanked open the drawer and took out a nasty-looking snub-nosed .38 belly gun. I popped open the cylinder, dumped the bullets on the floor, and tossed the gun away.

I reached for the arm of his oak swivel chair and spun him around to face me as I stepped back and pointed the .380 at his head.

"My god, Riordan, what the hell is this?" he shouted. "Why have you broken into my house? I'll have you arrested—"

I slapped him across the face with my gun hand. It wasn't a hard blow, but the barrel of the automatic slashed his cheek open, blood dripping on his shirt. I liked hitting him. Anger growled in my chest.

"We're going to talk," I said. "How well you do it decides whether you're still alive an hour from now."

He looked up, hiding his pain, and managed to work something like disdain onto his damaged face. "You're a fool, Riordan. Second-rate. You can't possibly hope to walk away from this. Okay. You want to talk, we'll talk. What about."

"The August 1971 bombing of the Joshua Stern Nuclear Reactor. The hired murders of Stephen Turner, Deborah Greene, Danny Schoen, Kyle Parman, and Mustafa Kemal.

The bomb that blew George Shields to meat in his own office."

"I really don't know what you're talking about, Riordan." He forced a laugh. His eyes narrowed. "I really don't. And even if I did, you can't prove anything against me."

I hit him again with the butt of the automatic, hard. The blow knocked him out of his chair. He sprawled on the floor. I hauled him off the floor and muscled his soft bulk back into his chair. Then I took him by the throat and forced his head up so that he was looking into my mad, drugged eyes.

"Listen to me, man," I said in a harsh, low voice. The voice was not my own, and I knew I was as crazy as he was, so far over the edge that I'd kill him if he didn't talk. "Don't fucking talk to me about proof. That's a legal word. It means nothing. There's no civilization here, no laws, no cops, no judges, and no rules. If you don't tell me what I want to know, I'm going to beat you to death. Slowly. And painfully."

I let him go. He slumped forward in the chair.

When he finally straightened up, I took the envelope with the two pictures inside of it from my pocket and tossed it on his desk. He opened it with trembling fingers and carefully straightened out the photographs, looking hard at the photograph of his younger self. He slowly turned it over and laid it facedown on his desk. When he picked up the second picture, the picture of the woman, he suddenly went pale, like an old man hearing the secrets of his youth being spoken aloud.

"Who was she, Darwin?" I asked softly.

"Her name was Margaret Cullen," he said slowly. "We were students together at Berkeley, in 1968. She was

beautiful. I fell in love with her the first time I saw her."
He shook his head. "I was an ugly, gawky engineering
student with pockets full of leaky pens and piles of books.
Why she loved me, I never knew."

I took a powerful little tape recorder out of my pocket
and set it on the table.

"Tell me about Joshua, Darwin. Tell me how the two of
you got involved."

"Meg was an activist," he said. She had joined SDS in
'68, just before Chicago. She organized a major demonstration in San Francisco in 1970. A couple of people had
been badly hurt, and they were going to file conspiracy
charges. So she went underground. I went with her. We
ended up wintering here, in this house, in the winter of
'70–71. George Shields owned it, and he hid us out." He
wiped blood from a face cut off his beard with his sleeve.
"The two of us were alone that whole winter; we never
needed anyone else. Christ, I wish I'd died then."

"What about the bombing?" I persisted.

"I was an engineer. I made the bombs we used at Fall
City. Then we wanted to go after a bigger target. The
Joshua power plant made plutonium for nuclear bombs.
Still does. It's a death machine. We just wanted to stop
it."

"You nearly poisoned a hundred-thousand people. The
plant almost had a meltdown."

"But we would have awakened the whole country to the
nuclear menace. It was worth it," he replied.

"Bullshit." Fanatics are always talking about the great-
est good. When you scratch the surface, you find that what
they like is the work. The games of cops and robbers. The
killing. Shit. "Who targeted the Joshua plant?"

"Paul Reid, from the Weather Bureau. They made up the fake names and college transcripts for us. That was all it took." He laughed, a surprisingly harsh sneer. "The fools made it easy for us. Once we were inside, working at the plant, it was simple." He stopped and wiped more of the blood off his face.

"I studied the designs and pinpointed the places to plant the charges," he continued. "Nobody saw us plant the first two." His voice slowed, and pain worked itself onto his face. "Meg was planting the third one herself because her job took her in and out of the control room a lot. She slipped in at the shift change. I was waiting outside in the corridor. When the shift chief ran into the control room, I was to far away to stop him. But then Meg . . . Meg had detonated the bombs."

He dropped his head into his arms and began to weep. I pulled his head up, more gently this time. He was fading. I had to keep him talking.

"How'd you get away, Darwin?"

"I ran. The bombs exploded, and I ran. In the confusion I got out of the generator plant and hid until morning. Then I walked over to the plutonium reprocessing complex. Hot-wired one of the government trucks. I dumped it in Pasco and just kept going. Three days later I was back underground in San Francisco.

"Why did you have Turner killed?"

"He knew . . . who I really was. We talked about the bombing just once, years ago. He swore that he would never say anything, that it was over and we should forget it, go on with our lives. But in the past few months he started dredging it up because the government was putting the plant back in plutonium production. He said we had an obligation to let people know how dangerous the plant was, how easily it had been hit. I told him no, he was crazy."

His voice rose, and flashes of life and anger began to show in his eyes. "Why should I have to take the blame now? That part of my life was finished. I had paid enough. More than enough."

"What about the others? Why kill Deborah Greene, or Kyle Parman? They weren't threatening you."

He looked at me obliquely out of the corners of his eyes. "I don't know who killed them, Riordan. Honestly."

My anger flared up again. I dragged him out of his chair and slammed him against the wall. I hit him in the face once, then again, popping the muscles in my arms and shoulders as I hit him. A reddish haze clouded my vision as I hit him in the body, again and again, hammering his ribs and belly with my fists. He couldn't cover up. He started to fall. My hands were slippery-wet from sweat and blood. I could no longer hold him up. His big, soft body slumped to the floor.

I nearly went down on top of him. I got my feet planted wide and pushed myself up, one hand on the wall, wheezing like an old machine.

I poked Darwin with my foot until he opened his eyes and looked at me.

"Let me tell you what I think happened," I said, staring coldly down at him. "I think you went home the day that Turner was shot and poured yourself a drink. You stared at that portrait on your wall. You thought back to the day, years before, when the bomb went off. You thought about Meg, dead instantly. You thought about panicking and running when she died. You thought about how you lay there in the desert grass crying, hoping to God they wouldn't find you. You thought about how all the others that were in on the bombing just walked away and went on to lead normal lives, lives with love in them, when all you've done for a dozen years is live with a name that's not your own, work yourself to exhaustion every day, and then go home to an empty house and a picture on the wall.''

I looked down at Darwin again. His eyes were half closed, and he stared away, seeing a far country in his mind. I prodded him with my toe.

"And that was when you decided to kill them all."

He nodded and closed his eyes.

I kicked him. "Say it."

"Yes."

There was a stirring at the door, and Bernstein walked into the room. He picked up the tape recorder and shut it off, then began rewinding the tape.

"We'll let them use this only if they have to," he said. He walked over to Darwin and put a hand under his chin, looking him over. Darwin's face was swollen and bleeding badly. His breath rasped. Bloody foam flecked his mouth. "Lousy," Bernstein said briskly. "Unprofessional. But enthusiastic."

He stepped away and reached in his pocket and pulled out a pint of bourbon and handed it to me.

He said, "I'll get that scum on the floor back to Seattle and turn him over to Ahlberg. They'll hold him until they can assemble the evidence. Now that they know who they're looking for they might be able to get him for George Shields's murder even without a confession. You go down into Cle Elum and get a room in a motel. Get some ice for your hands. You've probably broken them. Take a bath and try to get some sleep."

I opened the bourbon and tried to drink it. I swallowed some, but it tasted wrong and I gagged, spraying whiskey on the floor.

"What's wrong?" Bernstein asked sharply.

"I tortured him. And I very nearly killed him."

"That's what you had to do."

"Maybe. It's not so much what I did. It's what I am. I'm like him. As bad as he is."

I drank some more of the whiskey and walked to the door. I made it about halfway to the road before I fell to my knees and vomited sour whiskey and fresh blood on the ground.

CHAPTER 24

Four days later someone strangled Thomas Darwin with a towel in the infirmary of the county jail. Through a series of slightly suspicious mistakes, both guards and medical personnel happened to be out of the infirmary when it happened. No one was ever charged for his killing.

Shortly after Darwin's death, the Seattle police released major parts of the taped confession I had beaten out of him, including the details of the bombing at the Joshua Stern plant in 1971. There was a brief storm of protest over the government's cover-up of the bombing, but the news didn't light the fire that many people expected. The Nuclear Regulatory Commission and the Department of Energy issued bland reassurances that security measures at power plants and other nuclear facilities had been strengthened. The man who ordered the cover-up, a retired chairman of the old Atomic Energy Commission, placidly left his northern California farmhouse once a day and told the reporters camped outside to fuck off. One of his pigs had a litter while the story was current; the ex-chairman named the piglets for the reporters. That made more news than the bombing and coverup had.

I don't think Stephen Turner would have thought it was worth it.

In a way Darwin's death did me a lot of good. The Kittitas County prosecutor quietly dropped the assault charges she'd filed against me. The state bar association, courtesy of a lot of pressure from George Shields's father and his friends, dropped its investigation of me a few days later. I began to think it was finally over.

It was only halfway down in the fall, but it was surely winter in my heart. I stayed mostly sane and mostly sober, and dreamed of bright uncomplicated Mexican days to follow.

Kate recovered slowly from her wounds. She had the fragile, damaged look that she'd had right after her brother's death. This time it stayed with her, like an unwelcome ghost. I saw her every day, brought her books and the *Times* crossword, and hid my fears behind a line of bright chatter about the places in Mexico I'd take her. The words hung empty on the air. The books went mostly unread. She said very little.

A week or so after Darwin was killed the doctors said Kate could go home. Bernstein and I went to the hospital in the late afternoon, bearing the usual corny flowers and champagne. When we got there, Kate's room was empty.

A cheerful Fillipino admitting nurse stopped us on our way out. "Oh, Mr. Riordan," she said. "Mrs. Warden has already left with some friends. They want you to join them." She handed me a sealed envelope. I tore it open, trying to conceal my rising panic.

The note was printed in a precise, slanted hand. IT IS TIME FOR ANOTHER WALK, it said. THE PARK NORTH OF LAKE UNION. It was signed CRUZ.

Bernstein had read it over my shoulder. "Well, shit," he said. "Let's go see what the price is going to be."

"It's going to be high. But we're paying it."

When we got there, Cruz's limousine was already waiting at the eastern edge of Gasworks Park, near the old, corroded coal-gas works that gave the park its name. The city had left the gasworks standing as a sort of industrial sculpture, in weird contrast to the rolling green lawns of the park. Cruz had gotten out of the car and was standing beside the shell of the old plant, staring up at its columns.

I told Bernstein to take his position and walked over to see Cruz. He smiled as I approached, gesturing up at the gasworks. "I've tried and tried," he said, still smiling, "and I simply do not like this ancient coal still. Surely I lack artistic sophistication."

"You'd be in good company," I replied.

His eyes narrowed as he looked off at Bernstein making a casual half circle between the Lake Union shoreline and the kite-flyer's hills to the right of where Cruz and I stood. Cruz pointed in Bernstein's direction. "Your man?" he asked.

"Yes."

"Is he good?"

"Very."

"What are his instructions?"

"If this goes wrong, to get Mrs. Warden out alive."

"What about you?"

"I don't much give a shit about me. But whatever happens to me, happens to you."

"I see." He nodded, as if in agreement. "Let us walk."

We walked down toward Lake Union. It was a dark afternoon, and the clouds and the water were the color of old iron. A fine mist began to fall. One by one, the last of the hard-core kite-flyers reeled in their paper and balsa contraptions and headed for home.

"The thing I wasn't able to figure out," I began, "was where you fit into this mess. At first I thought you might just be protecting Danny Schoen. When Raines killed him, that didn't make sense anymore. And a punk like Danny Schoen didn't seem important enough for you to risk involving yourself personally. But then Darwin came into the picture. Now, how does a guy like Darwin, an anxious computer jock, find an assassin like Raines? Not through the want ads. Answer: he goes to somebody with connections. Somebody with power. Somebody like you, Cruz."

He said nothing. I pushed on.

"Assume I'm right. How does Darwin pay you? Not with money. You take in maybe a million a week, maybe more. You've got so much money flowing in every month, it isn't real anymore; it's an abstraction. No way can Darwin come up with enough bucks to tempt you.

"So, what does he do? He trades. Darwin's company-designed computer software for banks and insurance companies and oil companies. Companies with a lot of accounts, a lot of transactions to keep track of. Money's an abstraction for them, too. It's just one electronic pulse chasing around after another in the guts of their computers. Darwin's software runs those computers." I stopped and looked at him. His narrow, hard face was calm, dispassionate. He must have been hell at poker.

"One of the biggest problems in the crime business is handling money. It's a tremendous hassle to move that cash around, and it's also the point where you're most vulnerable. If the cops can't get you, maybe the IRS can. But those big companies would make damn-fine money Laundromats, wouldn't they? Spread the cash out in a thousand, ten-thousand little accounts and move it gradually through a company's own accounts. If the accounts balanced, they might never know. With access to the computer systems and the right designs to the software, it would be easy. How close, Mr. Cruz?"

He smiled again. "A bit sketchy, but essentially correct. I confess to underestimating you. You even maneuvered me into having Darwin killed, admittedly the appropriate response to his actions."

"I don't follow you."

His voice got tough. "Don't pretend innocence, Riordan. You must have known that once Darwin confessed to his own crimes, I could not trust him to stay silent about his dealings with me. He could trade that information for a reduction of his sentence, perhaps even freedom. You knew I would have to kill him."

"You assume too much," I replied.

"Perhaps. I will tell you this much, Mr. Riordan. Darwin did come to me. He told me that he needed assistance. He mentioned no names. I arranged for Mr. Raines's services. When I found out that Danny Schoen had been killed, I tried to stop Raines. By then Darwin was paying him directly. And I had lost control." He sighed. "I should have prevented this. I do not like injuries to by-standers. I have apologized to Mrs. Warden.''

"I'm not sure it would have made any difference. What happens now, Mr. Cruz?''

"We need an agreement, Mr. Riordan. We need to make one today. Or I cannot permit any of you to leave this place. Even though you might very well succeed in killing me.''

"All right," I said. "An agreement. What are your terms?''

"Your silence. With Mrs. Warden's life as the guarantee.''

"You'll have to clean up whatever trail that exists tying you to Darwin. Otherwise I could go down on obstruction of justice charges.''

"It is already done.''

"Then, we agree.'' I surprised myself. I didn't even hesitate.

"It is best, Mr. Riordan. I believe there is nothing more to say. I wish you well.'' Cruz turned and walked quietly away over the damp grass meadow.

I wondered if it was his own serenity or just indifference that allowed him to face life and death so casually. Maybe there is no distinction between the two.

I found Kate down at the edge of the water, looking at a sign on a chain-link fence that blocked off part of the park. A sign on the fence said that toxic chemicals from the coal plant had leached through the clay cap that had been laid down over the old piles of plant spoil and ash. Now the topsoil and the water of the lake were both contaminated.

She turned as I walked up and put both my hands in hers. She started to speak but stopped. Her eyes slipped away from mine.

"It's all right," I said, forcing a smile. "I know you're going away. Come on, let's walk around the other side of the hill. You can see the city better from over there."

As we walked Kate asked, "Why did Cruz take me from the hospital? He made it very clear I had no choice. Was he connected to this?"

"He was tied into it. He took you to show me and you that he could hurt you or kill you anytime he wanted."

"But why? Was my brother—?"

"No. Not at all. Your brother had nothing to do with Cruz, didn't know that Cruz would be involved. Don't think badly of your brother, Kate. All he tried to do was find a way to have something good come out of crimes he'd committed years ago. In a way, that's what we all tried to do."

She nodded soberly. "What did you and Cruz talk about?" she asked.

"Our lives. I made a deal with him. We don't talk about his involvement. In return he lets us live."

She reached out and caressed my face with the back of her hand. "That bothers you a lot, doesn't it?"

"Not much," I replied. "I went outside my own rules when I beat that confession out of Thomas Darwin." I took a deep breath and looked at the lights shining through the dark afternoon from the big buildings downtown. A mirror image of the city reflected off the surface of the water. "You see, Kate, I've always believed in law, believed that even if it might not give you truth it would eventually give you justice. I always expected others to follow the rules. When I was a prosecutor, I would break bad agents, agents who beat suspects, the way you'd break a match. Toss the pieces away and never think about it.

213

But when my own time came, I wasn't up to it. When I had to know if Darwin was guilty, I used the oldest technique in the world. I tortured him.''

I shrugged. "My problem. By making a deal with Cruz, all of us go on living. For me, that's enough. What about you, Kate?''

She took one of my hands in both of hers. "I'm responsible for what happened after Steve's death. I know what Darwin told you, but I am. The pressure I put on him made it easy for him to keep killing.'' She closed her eyes and shut them tight, as though trying to close out the world.

I said, "You can't be responsible for what other people do, Kate. They have the choices to make.''

"So did I.''

Nothing I could say would change her mind. The words had to be better. Or come from someone else.

I put my arms around her. She felt still and awkward in my arms. Fearing the answer I would get, I asked, "What will you do now, Kate?''

"Do what rich women do in romance novels,'' she said with an ironic smile. "Flee. My mother owned a house in London, a row house in Chelsea, near the Thames. It's mine now. That's where I'll live. I'll be one of those slightly aimless people you see in the British Museum, sketching the Elgin marbles. Or reading a novel at teatime in Harrods.''

"I could be there,'' I said hesitantly. "Whenever you say.''

"No,'' she said, her smile gone. "Please, Matthew, no. I think I love you in spite of what you did. What we did.

Or maybe because of what we did. But when I see you I see—'' She lost the rest.

"Katie, it's okay," I said softly. "I understand."

She nodded and kissed me. Then she turned and was gone.

Bernstein hung around a few days longer, his mind happily focused on the ways of all flesh and the size of the certified check forwarded by Kate's family lawyer. I tried to catch him during the pauses in his revels—Bernstein is ethnically Jewish, but a practicing pagan—and even then he was not much interested in serious talk.

"Okay," he said finally. "What you did to Darwin was wrong. So what? He killed five people. I think you had no choice. You think that what you did makes you the same as some Chilean colonel with greased-back hair and thumbscrews in a basement room. That's not right. You're missing an important difference."

"What's the difference?" I asked him.

"You grieve," he explained.

That was as much absolution as I was ever going to get. When Bernstein left, I cleaned up my cases, cleared my calendar, and bought one ticket on Mexicana, for Manzanillo, with an open return.

About the Author

Frederick Huebner is an attorney who lives in Seattle, Washington. THE JOSHUA SEQUENCE is his first novel.

Attention Mystery and Suspense Fans

Do you want to complete your collection
of mystery and suspense stories
by some of your favorite authors?
John D. MacDonald, Helen MacInnes,
Dick Francis, Amanda Cross, Ruth
Rendell, Alistar MacLean, Erle Stanley
Gardner, Cornell Woolrich, among many
others, are included in Ballantine/
Fawcett's new Mystery Brochure.

For your FREE Mystery Brochure, fill in the
coupon below and mail it to:

**Ballantine/Fawcett Books
Education Department — MB
201 East 50th Street
New York, NY 10022**

Name_____

Address_____

City_____State_____Zip____.____

12   TA-94